of speed, he reached the [...] re were several small kegs of black powder. He drew his Colt and used it to crack the board cover when the noisy dancers were at a peak in their chanting. He spread the granules all over the ammo boxes, then made a track of it to the rear. There would not be much time between his lighting the powder and a hell of an explosion.

One chance was all he would get to set off his surprise. The Indians at the nearby fire were whooping it up. Slocum drew out a match, struck it, and touched the flame to the powder. A small flicker, then the trail flared and he ran as hard as he could. Not looking back, he reached the horses when the blast went skyward. He mounted his animal, who was panicked by the blinding, ear-shattering blast. They swept westward under the stars toward their own camp. When Slocum looked back and saw the exploding rounds of ammo fill the night sky with fireworks, he smiled. *Sorry, Bull Elk, you ain't using those bullets.*

DON'T MISS THESE
ALL-ACTION WESTERN SERIES
FROM THE BERKLEY PUBLISHING GROUP

THE GUNSMITH by J. R. Roberts
Clint Adams was a legend among lawmen, outlaws, and ladies. They called him . . . the Gunsmith.

LONGARM by Tabor Evans
The popular long-running series about Deputy U.S. Marshal Long—his life, his loves, his fight for justice.

SLOCUM by Jake Logan
Today's longest-running action Western. John Slocum rides a deadly trail of hot blood and cold steel.

BUSHWHACKERS by B. J. Lanagan
An action-packed series by the creators of Longarm! The rousing adventures of the most brutal gang of cutthroats ever assembled—Quantrill's Raiders.

DIAMONDBACK by Guy Brewer
Dex Yancey is Diamondback, a Southern gentleman turned con man when his brother cheats him out of the family fortune. Ladies love him. Gamblers hate him. But nobody pulls one over on Dex . . .

WILDGUN by Jack Hanson
The blazing adventures of mountain man Will Barlow—from the creators of Longarm!

TEXAS TRACKER by Tom Calhoun
Meet J. T. Law: the most relentless—and dangerous—manhunter in all Texas. Where sheriffs and posses fail, he's the best man to bring in the most vicious outlaws—for a price.

JAKE LOGAN

SLOCUM AND THE DEADWOOD DEAL

JOVE BOOKS, NEW YORK

THE BERKLEY PUBLISHING GROUP
Published by the Penguin Group
Penguin Group (USA) Inc.
375 Hudson Street, New York, New York 10014, USA
Penguin Group (Canada), 10 Alcorn Avenue, Toronto, Ontario M4V 3B2, Canada
(a division of Pearson Penguin Canada Inc.)
Penguin Books Ltd., 80 Strand, London WC2R 0RL, England
Penguin Group Ireland, 25 St. Stephen's Green, Dublin 2, Ireland (a division of Penguin Books Ltd.)
Penguin Group (Australia), 250 Camberwell Road, Camberwell, Victoria 3124, Australia
(a division of Pearson Australia Group Pty. Ltd.)
Penguin Books India Pvt. Ltd., 11 Community Centre, Panchsheel Park, New Delhi—110 017, India
Penguin Group (NZ), Cnr. Airborne and Rosedale Roads, Albany, Auckland 1310, New Zealand
(a division of Pearson New Zealand Ltd.)
Penguin Books (South Africa) (Pty.) Ltd., 24 Sturdee Avenue, Rosebank, Johannesburg 2196,
South Africa

Penguin Books Ltd., Registered Offices: 80 Strand, London WC2R 0RL, England

SLOCUM AND THE DEADWOOD DEAL

A Jove Book / published by arrangement with the author

PRINTING HISTORY
Jove edition / April 2005

ISBN: 0-515-13933-5

JOVE®
Jove Books are published by The Berkley Publishing Group,
a division of Penguin Group (USA) Inc.,
375 Hudson Street, New York, New York 10014.
JOVE is a registered trademark of Penguin Group (USA) Inc.
The "J" design is a trademark belonging to Penguin Group (USA) Inc.

PRINTED IN THE UNITED STATES OF AMERICA

10 9 8 7 6 5 4 3 2 1

1

Slocum wiped the beads of sweat off his upper lip with his curled forefinger. Those two jaspers bellied down somewhere in the sagebrush at the base of the hill wanted him dead. He could see their saddled horses grazing to the side. Nothing in his hearing but some shy-poke bird making a mating call, and the wind. Who in the hell were they?

The horse he'd rode in on, a big blue roan, standing off in the draw, raised his head up and looked in their direction between snatched mouthfuls of the dried bunch grass. Roan wasn't going anywhere—trained to ground tie, he would be there when the time came to ride out. That would be if Slocum lived that long.

Then another wild barrage of rifle shots went zinging over Slocum's head and he hugged the ground harder. Damn them shooters. The Colt in his sweaty hand was ready, but so far there'd been no opportunity to answer them. When he breathed, the pungent aroma of the sagebrush filled his nostrils. These hard heads down there were out to kill him.

"Throw your hands up!" one of them ordered.

"Who in the hell are you?"

"Come on, Ellsworth, you know who we are." Ellsworth? Aw, hell. He gazed up at the azure sky for help. They'd made a big mistake. How could he ever convince them they had the wrong guy? Better keep his head down until he could persuade them he wasn't Ellsworth. They acted like they were playing their game for keeps.

"That ain't my name," he shouted over the hard wind. "You ain't got Ellsworth up here."

"Bullshit! We know who you are."

"Listen, my name's Slocum."

"Slocum? You ain't never been to Bender's Gap?"

"Hell, no." He waited, listening for their reply. While he couldn't make out their words, the two were obviously talking over the matter of his identity. He'd been called lots of names, but never an Ellsworth. All he knew about the town by that name was that it sat thirty miles or so west of Abilene, Kansas and over two hundred miles across the sunflower state from where he was at.

"You sure as shit looked like Ellsworth."

"Well, I sure as shit ain't him. What did this Ellsworth fellow do?" He listened closely for their reply.

"Messed with Henry's wife."

"Messed?"

"More than messed. He raped her."

"I don't even know Henry, let alone his wife."

"We'll call it a truce then," the voice called back.

"No tricks or someone's going to die." He wanted them to be certain he wasn't walking into a trap or they'd pay with their lives.

"If'n you ain't Ellsworth, there ain't no need in that."

"Well, I damn sure ain't him."

The cease-fire was shaky at best. After several

more shouting matches, Slocum rose, and so did the other two. Then both sides, still armed, advanced on each other.

They halted twenty feet apart. The .44 in his fist and pressed against his right leg, Slocum looked them over. The short one had yellow hair like wheat straw that stuck out from under his weathered felt hat. The tall one wore a beard and mustache. He looked like a willow pole with a high-crown Boss of the Plains hat on top of his head.

"I'm Henry," the short one said. Late teens or early twenties, Slocum figured him, hardly more than a boy.

"I'm Buster."

"Slocum's mine."

"He ain't Ellsworth," Henry said, looking disappointed.

Buster agreed with a defeated nod. "You sure looked like him the first time we spotted you."

"Good, that's settled. I'm looking for a man named Steward. You two know him?"

"Joe or Josh?"

"They both live around here?"

"Yeah, they're brothers and boy, do they hate each other."

Slocum wiped off his mouth with the back of his hand. All he could recall about the letter in the mail was that it was signed J. Steward. He holstered the Colt, shifted the harness on his hip and drew a deep breath.

"Where is the closest Steward?"

"About five miles north. S Bar T Brand. That's Josh, meanest man in Clare County, Kansas."

"Good, I'll find him. Who's this Ellsworth you mistook me for?"

"Randolph Ellsworth. He's the biggest adulterer in the county."

"Must be bad."

"Bad? I'd bet there are over a hundred men who'd pay you good money for his corpse."

"Including you—"

Henry's eyes narrowed and he drew his breath up his nose. "I'd shoot him in a minute."

"He's a smooth talker, mister. Yes, sir, he can talk women into anything. Giving him their egg money, giving him their husband's clothes, even crawling in bed with him. He's a real dandy," Buster said, and shook his head ruefully.

"Sumbitch," Henry swore and spat tobacco to the side. "I get him in the sights of this here Spencer, he's dead."

"Well, next time be sure that it's him that you're shooting at," Slocum said and started to leave to get his horse.

"Yeah," Buster agreed and Henry nodded.

Slocum left the pair and hiked up the hill for the roan. He thought he'd better check out the first Steward. No telling which one it was. He'd received the letter general delivery forwarded to Socorro, New Mexico. Lucky it even found him. This Steward claimed he needed some help and even wrote that Bart James said if Steward could find Slocum, he might come help out. Bart James was an old friend who, last Slocum had heard about him, was on the dodge from the law too.

Slocum rode in under the faded S Bar T sign and headed for the distant headquarters. Some stock dogs heralded a welcome when he rode in the ranch yard and a man came out on the porch. He was gray-headed with dark eyes that registered his impatience. His brown pants were patched and his wool vest tattered at the edges. Obviously he spent little money on his attire.

"Guess you're looking for a meal," the man said.

"Slocum's my name." He patted the roan on the neck to settle him.

"Well, Slocum. You can just ride out of here. I don't

feed hands riding the chuck line and I don't need any help."

"Guess you've answered all my questions," Slocum said and picked up the reins to leave. No need to ask him where his brother lived. A man that inhospitable wouldn't give him the time of day, let alone any information.

"And tell the rest of those lazy rider friends of yours to stay the hell off my ranch too."

A young woman stepped out on the porch. His daughter? Early twenties, willowy figure with a wide leather belt that cinched in her hour-glass figure, and long blond hair. Her good looks caught Slocum's breath.

"Who is he?" she asked Steward.

"Says his name is Slocum, Judy."

"Oh, good day." She smiled pleasantly as if to make up for his rudeness.

He tipped his hat. "Pleased to meet you, ma'am."

"I told you to get the hell out of here. You know damn good and well that I don't put up with chuck line riders on my place."

"Did you ask him his business?" she asked, moving to hold a porch post with one hand, her blue eyes dancing with a deep look that made Slocum wonder about her.

"Good day, Miss Judy," he said, tipping his hat and turning the roan.

"—and don't come back!" Steward said from behind her.

At sundown, he reached a crossroads store and bought some jerky, cheese and crackers to feast upon. The clerk wanted to talk and soon filled him in on Joe Steward's location, told him all about Josh Steward's usual bad disposition and stinginess, and with bleary eyes talked wistfully about Judy Steward.

"Why, that girl is prettier than any queen," the boy of perhaps eighteen swooned.

"Nice looking," Slocum agreed, washing his dry food down with a bottle of sarsaparilla from the water cooler, a canvas-covered box they kept wet so the evaporation chilled the drinks inside.

"Nice looking?" The boy shook his head in disbelief. "Man, it eats my guts up just looking at her."

"She engaged?"

"Engaged? Why that old man would kill you if you even spoke a word to her."

Slocum nodded and took another of his cheese-and-cracker sandwiches. One thing for sure, she'd be a nice bed full, from what he had seen of her body. This poor boy had a bad case on her.

"You know a guy named Ellsworth?"

"Ellsworth?" The boy's eyes flew open. "You know him?"

"I've heard of him." Slocum waved the bottle at the clerk so he could give himself a second to swallow his food.

"I heard," the youth dropped his voice, "he's got a tool bigger than a stud horse."

"Hmm. He must be big."

"I overheard two farmers' wives talking about him right here in this store. One said to the other he was so big she couldn't breathe when he stuck it in her."

"That's something. I guess it's a wonder he ain't been shot already—I mean him messing around with other men's wives and all."

The youth nodded. "He's been lucky."

"Guess he has been that all right. I need to find this Joe Steward. Better get moving."

"Come back by," the clerk said, taking up the broom and starting to sweep the floor.

"I may," Slocum said.

• • •

He found Joe's place in the twilight. A neat enough farm in a big patch of ripe wheat. The stock dogs met him, barking in a friendly way at him and the roan.

"Howdy," the man said and came out on the porch.

"Slocum's my name." He could see lots of resemblance in the two men.

"Joe Steward's mine, get off your horse. What can I do for you?"

Do for me? Obviously this brother didn't recognize him either. Slocum dropped heavily from the saddle. Which Steward was it? He rubbed the stubble on his upper lip with his forefinger and wondered what he was into.

"Come on in, my wife has some coffee."

"All right," Slocum agreed and loosened the cinch.

"Who's here?" a short woman with some gray in her hair asked, coming to stand in the doorway.

"A gentleman named Slocum."

"Oh, how nice," she said. She made a curtsy and went back inside the lighted entrance.

The house was wood-framed, a sign of prosperity in western Kansas, where most of the residents lived in soddies. Slocum took off his hat when he came into the living room and nodded to her as she arrived with a tray of coffee cups and pastry.

"You a cattle buyer, Mr. Slocum?"

"Yes, ma'am," he said, feeling that was as good as anything else. "Actually I am looking for grass to graze for a corporation."

"Big guys going to own it all," Steward complained. "Have a seat." He indicated the straight-back chairs at the table.

"Guess so," Slocum agreed and thanked her for his coffee and the sweet bread she put on a plate before him.

They made small talk like most people did when they had visitors and they asked him a lot about the country he came from.

"Isn't near as much grass in New Mexico as here, but except for up in the mountains they have much milder winters."

"There's always somewhere better," Steward said. "A place where the watermelons get too big to haul in a wagon or one turnip will fill a bushel basket."

Darling Steward smiled at her husband. Slocum guessed her to be mid-thirties—no children. They probably wanted some, but obviously after ten years of marriage they had not been blessed with any. The three of them talked into the night and at last Steward said he was sleepy and showed Slocum to a small tool room with a cot, by the barn.

Slocum thanked the man, promised to be up by breakfast. Then he put the roan in the corral with Steward's draft horses, where his pony had hay and water. His bedroll laid out, he took off his gun belt and boots, then lay on top of the covers. Still too warm to need a blanket over him, he rested on his back. Sleep avoided him so he listened to the insects sizzle in the night.

Why did someone write to him for help—then not claim they knew him? Perhaps they were absentminded. Still, it looked like he'd ridden a long ways for nothing.

"You asleep, Mr. Slocum?"

He could make out Darling standing in the doorway and looking back toward the starlight-washed house.

"No, ma'am. What can I do for you?" He swung his legs over the side, sat up and combed back his hair with his fingers.

"I had to talk to someone."

"Sure, come sit on the cot."

"Oh, no. I'll just stand here—I mean in the doorway. I hated to trouble you."

"You aren't any trouble."

"I wanted to thank you for stopping by. I loved your stories of New Mexico. I'll never get to go see those places. But tonight I was there. You made a foolish woman very pleased."

"Foolish?" He could see her silhouette backed to the door frame. The pearly light outlined her petite figure.

"I guess I've always dreamed a lot."

"Oh, about what?"

"Oh, traveling to different places. Seeing and meeting different people. It won't ever happen, you know, because I'll die right here on this farm. But thanks for fulfilling some of my dreams."

"Anything else I can do for you?" he asked.

"Oh, no, I just wanted to thank you. Good night, Mr. Slocum."

He watched her hurry off to the house. Lost her nerve after she got out there, he decided with a knowing smile. He lay back down, closed his eyes and thought about what she'd look like undressed, then he went to sleep. Who had written that letter needing his help . . . ?

2

Sunup came in golden spears across the eastern horizon. They shot over the land of rolling hills—actually, they were more like waves in the sea of brown and green grass. Steward's yellow wheat field looked ready to harvest, waist high and heavy heads swaying in the cool morning gusts. His crop land fit like a patched quilt into the flow of the country.

Slocum washed himself off to the waist at the horse tank and dried off with a sack towel from his own things. Steward came by with a bucket to milk the brindle cow. He mumbled "Good morning" in his passing and went on to the gate where the jersey waited, making low moos.

"Wife's got coffee on. Go on up there. I'll be along."

"Thanks." Slocum put on his shirt, then his vest. The weathered Stetson on his head, he set out for the house. Putting his hat on a peg, he ducked under the lintel and entered the house, heavy with the aroma of fresh baking sourdough.

"Good morning," she said and smiled at him. In her ironed white apron, she hustled about her range and dry sink getting breakfast ready.

"Sure smells good in here."

"Baking bread is a wonderful thing to sniff in the morning. Summertime I try to bake all my things in the cool part of the day."

"Smart idea," he said, taking a seat at the table.

"You have a wife, Mr. Slocum?"

"No, ma'am."

"You think you ever will?"

"I guess everyone would like to have a place, a wife and a home to say is mine."

She turned to look at him and nodded she had heard him, then turned back to rolling out pie dough. "But then you'd have to give up seeing all the new corners of the country."

"That can get old too."

She glanced up at the ceiling. "I imagine after a while anything is drudgery. Next week the harvest crew will be here with the reaper to cut the wheat. I'll be cooking twenty-four hours a day."

She flopped the dough over a tin pie pan and cut the excess off the edges with a sharp knife. "The company will be fun, but the extra work will soon get old."

"Are there any more Stewards beside Joe and his brother in the country?"

She turned from her work and looked mildly at him. "No, why do you ask?"

"Just wondered."

"Actually there's only five Stewards in the country. Joe and me, his older brother, Josh, Steven, his son and his daughter, Judy."

"How old are Josh's children?"

"Steve and Judy? Oh, he's about twenty-five and she's twenty-one this year. We don't ever visit anymore. Joe and Josh had a terrible fight several years ago and they can't stand to be around each other ever since then." She brought the granite pot over and poured him coffee in a tin cup.

"What about—the fight, I mean?"

"Josh accused Joe of taking more than his share of a deal." She shook her head. "Joe never took anything wasn't his—but the bad words have been spoken and the two avoid each other at all costs. Caused us to join the Lutheran church, because Josh goes to the Methodist one."

Slocum nodded as he blew on the coffee and stared at the big deer rack over the fireplace. Family break-ups weren't unusual and became irreparable before they were over. He still had no idea about the identity of the *J* on that letter.

"You going scouting grass today?"

"I guess. What's the name of the next town?"

"Bender's Gap is about five miles north of here."

"Very big place?"

She shook her head, busy placing dry apple slices in her pie pan. "Two bars, two stores, a saddle-maker, harness shop, and blacksmith. Oh, yes—" She searched about to be certain they were alone, then in a whisper said, "Miss Emma's house. You know what I mean?"

He nodded and then heard her husband coming with the milk.

"How's the cow?" she asked when he came thorough the door.

"Fine, still giving milk," he said, putting the pail on the dry sink. Behind her back, he shook his head at her. "How else could a cow be?"

"I was merely making conversation."

"Well, she's fine." He poured himself coffee and came over to the table. "How are you this morning?"

"Doing better with this fine coffee." Slocum smiled at him and toasted him with the tin cup.

"Yeah, it sure beats drinking burnt barley."

"We have neighbors drink that," she put in. "Served some to Joe for coffee one time and he about got sick on it."

"They poor folks?"

"No, they're Swedes," Joe said, "and they're too cheap to buy real coffee, so they say they can't tell the difference."

"You don't know any other Stewards besides us and Josh's, do you?" she asked her husband.

"Nope, why?"

"I was just asking," Slocum said to settle the matter.

"My brother lives south of here."

"I met him yesterday."

"I can tell you were impressed, he was so friendly."

"Must of been the wrong one, the one I met wasn't friendly at all," Slocum said and they all laughed.

After breakfast, he thanked them for their hospitality and offered to pay for his keep. After they refused to take his money he went and saddled his horse.

Before noontime he reached Bender's Gap or at least the outskirts. There on the prairie he came upon a two-story clapboard building sitting all by itself a quarter mile from the cluster of buildings that he assumed was the town. No yard or lawn around a large house and an empty double hitchrail in front of the porch.

A young woman appeared in the upstairs window. She stuck a shapely bare leg out the opening and then ducked under the top half of the frame so she was astraddle the sill and hanging outside.

"Morning, cowboy," she said. As her dark hair was swirled in her face by the wind, she swept it back with one hand; the other one rested on her exposed knee. "You wouldn't be needing a little now, would you?"

He tipped his hat and grinned big. "Got some business in town. But maybe later. What's your name?"

"Sweet Irish Rose." She looked at him provocatively. "I might be better right now."

"Thanks, but business before pleasure."

"See you later. You won't regret it."

He watched her draw the shift up and expose her shapely thigh, then with both her breasts about to fly out of the top, she cupped them from underneath as she leaned out the window. "You better come back and see me."

"I'll try," he said, waved and rode on.

The bartender in the first saloon had not heard of any other Stewards and the amplebodied woman behind the second bar shook her head. "Nope, there ain't no more."

Then the man at the small post office looked at the stamp on the envelope with his glasses. "Yeah, that letter was mailed from here. Whatcha need to know?"

"Nothing, just curious."

"Oh, by the way, you have a letter here. You are J. Slocum, aren't you?"

"Sure. How long's it been here?"

The man, looking over his glasses, sorted through the stack of general delivery letters. "I can tell you when I read the date it was stamped. Right here. Says do not forward. Hold for him. Let's see, mailed at Henson, Kansas two weeks ago."

"Where's Henson?"

"Thirty miles south."

Slocum nodded, took the envelope and went outside to read it, despite the obviously curious clerk.

Dear Slocum,

Please be patient. Stay close to town and I will contact you in the next few days. Sorry I must be so mys-

terious, but certain conditions in my life make that
necessary. I do have a large problem and need your
help.

Sincerely yours,
J. Steward

Nothing more. He tapped the folded letter on his other hand. No answer except to wait for the party. Perhaps he should stick around and see the outcome. He wiped the stubble around his mouth with his calloused hand—there was a small barbershop across the street, maybe he'd start there with a shave, haircut and bath—then perhaps a roll in the hay with the wild Irish Rose or with one of her "sisters."

A rotund fellow, the barber in Bender's Gap put down his Denver newspaper when Slocum walked in.

"Aaron Riggins is my name," he said, shaking out his striped sheet and showing him the chair.

"Slocum's mine." He climbed up into the fancy chrome leather seat.

"Oh, not John Doe or Joe Smith?" Riggins pinned on the covering around Slocum's throat.

"Slocum."

"Well, Slocum, we'll whittle a little on your hair."

"Shave and a bath too."

"My, my, that will come to over the grand total of thirty cents."

"I'm the big spender this afternoon," Slocum said

"What brings a gentleman like you to this desolate burg anyway?"

"Said they had the best barber in the West here."

"Well, bless their soul," Riggins said and went to clacking his scissors. "I could have been a banker, but I decided that I'd take people's excess hair, not clip their money." He laughed at his joke and Slocum nodded in approval.

Ten more corny jokes later, Riggins snapped the sheet off him and smiled. "Bath next?" The barber bent at the waist and used his arm to point to the curtained door in the back.

Slocum agreed and followed his directions. The dimly lighted back room smelled of old bathwater and soap. A little light shone in from one grimy small window in the bathhouse that held three tin tubs. Riggins fed wood into the roaring heater in the back, assuring him the water would be ready in no time.

"You can undress." He turned and listened to a small bell ringing over the door. "Better go see who that is. Maybe my second cash customer of the day."

Slocum agreed and sat down on the bench to toe off his boots. He removed his holey socks next and piled them on the boot tops. Then he took off his shirt. How long would the water be heating?

Riggins came rushing back, tested the vat, pronounced it ready and bailed out two pails to dump into the first tub. When it was half full, he excused himself and rushed out with, "Have a nice bath, sir."

Slocum removed his pants and underwear, found the soap and stepped into the tub. The water was tepid but it would work. He scoured away two inches of grime and his nose was soon full of the soap's pine-tar aroma. He could hear Riggins talking away—telling the same jokes to his new customer in the shop.

"I'll be there to rinse you off in a minute," the barber assured him from the doorway.

No rush, Slocum decided as he slumped down in the tub with his snow-white knees sticking up. He was waiting for J. Steward to show up.

3

"Where's the best place to eat in this town?" Slocum asked the buxom woman behind the bar in Harry's Saloon.

She looked up from polishing a glass and flipped the limp brown hair from her full face. "Ain't got one. Help yourself to the free lunch."

"No, I mean like meat, potatoes, bread." He was tired of cold boiled eggs, head cheese, moldy cheddar, mustard and stale crackers.

"There ain't no such place. You'd starve to death running a café in this dried-up burg. Hell"—she set down the glass, gave her boobs under the dress a shove up and waddled over to where he stood to put her sausage-like arms on the bar—"if I didn't turn a trick or two a week I'd lose this place. Business is slow enough this afternoon." She gave a toss of her head to the rear. "You wouldn't want to go in back and get you any nooky would you?"

He never broke a smile. "Not this afternoon."

"Come back." She began to roll a cigarette in her short fingers then looked up at him with sleepy brown eyes. "You ain't had any real pussy till you've had a fat woman."

He finished his beer, set the glass down and nodded in agreement. "You're probably right."

She nodded, smiled, smugly intent on her rolling business, then she licked the cigarette shut with the tip of her red tongue. A torpedo-headed match struck smoke that soon escaped the edges of her lips and she moved it away with a cough. "I ain't never failed to satisfy any man that climbed on me." More coughs.

He paid her and left. Outside in the too bright hot sun, he wondered where was this J. Steward? Maybe he'd throw a fling at Miss Emma's. At the hitchrail, he tightened the cinch and swung into the saddle to head that way. No sense wasting such a great day, he decided, looking at the cloudless azure sky. Besides, the company of a frisky woman beat his own any day.

There were two ponies standing hipshot at the rack when he rode up to the establishment, nondescript bay mustangs that had been ridden hard to get there and the floury road-dust was caked to their knees. Their shoulders were white-flecked with dried salt. Both looked grateful to be there and Slocum wondered about their riders. He studied the open windows upstairs and the hem of the lace curtains flowing out of them in the stiff wind, keeping the afternoon Kansas temperature from rising any higher.

He dismounted heavily, removed his spurs and hung them on the horn, then he loosened the girth. Over the stiff wind, he could hear the player piano tinkling away. Then the yahoo yells of someone inside raising hell with some loud-laughing sister.

To focus his vision in the dim light, he stood in the open doorway for a long moment. He made eye contact with an unshaven hard case of medium height who released the dove under his arm. Except for the gal with her back to them pumping the player and singing "Camptown Races," everyone in the room stood frozen.

"That you Charlie Hash?" Slocum asked, his body tingling with the electricity of being ready for anything.

"Yeah, Slocum, what the hell're you going to do about it?"

They stood five paces apart, face to face, hands poised like coiled rattlers ready to strike for their holsters. Silent doves with worrisome looks in their eyes quickly melted aside to the room's walls in their wary concern. Only the wind sweeping through the open house and the rustle of the curtains could be heard.

"Where did I see you last?" Hash asked.

"Tularosa?"

"Yeah, you had that good-looking widow woman—" Hash pointed his finger gun-like at Slocum to make his point. "She was sure damn pretty."

"Nice lady."

"Well, tell you what, I'll buy you a drink and you can tell me all about her."

"No," Slocum said as the tension drained from his muscles. "I'll buy you one and you can tell me why you ain't got one of these good-lookers corraled and up in bed with you right now."

Both men straightened and advanced toward each other. They shook hands, looked each other over and nodded in approval.

"Well, I'll be a sumbitch, two minutes ago I'd thought you two was cold-hearted enemies," the dark-haired sister said, coming back into the room.

"We are, darling," Hash said, pouring whiskey in two glasses on the small bar. "But we ain't letting it stand in the way of our getting us a good piece of ass—right, Slocum?"

"Right," Slocum said and raised the glass to toast them.

The four girls came back in, prancing and dancing. One took a seat at the piano and soon the tinkling music began to fill the room.

"What've you been doing since Tularosa?" Slocum asked as both of them leaned on the bar and considered the brown liquor in their glasses.

"Went to Cheyenne. A guy promised me a deal up there but it fell through. Been looking since then." Hash gave a head toss. "Micheals is already upstairs with one of them. He's had him a big hard-on the last hundred miles."

Slocum nodded.

"Where've you been?"

"Socorro. You remember Burt Hayes?"

"Yeah."

"He has a saloon there. I dealt some cards for him."

"Getting tougher and tougher to find work anywhere anymore."

Slocum agreed and smiled down at the redheaded dove with her tit stuck in the crook of his right arm. "Getting harder and harder all the time."

She reached down in front of him and ran her palm familiarly over the bulge in his pants. "It sure is, honey. Why don't we go upstairs and sink that dude in a real doughnut."

"Hated to get into it," Hash said, like he was thinking about something else and shook his head looking full of regret.

"What's that?" Slocum asked, slipping his arm over the redhead's shoulder and drawing her against him with his attention centered on Hash. He could feel she had on something like a stiff undergarment beneath the shift she wore.

"Me getting into this damn outlaw business."

Slocum knew and nodded his head. "Tough decision."

Hash nodded and threw down his whiskey. "Bad one to make."

"Better enjoy yourself while you can here."

Then Hash agreed and splashed more whiskey in his glass. Later, when he offered another fill-up, Slocum shook his head and grinned down at the attachment hugging his waist and pressing her pubic bone against his leg.

Worked up, he drew a sharp breath up his nose. "Let's go," he said to her over the clanking player piano and the shouting of the two girls polka-ing around the room together.

She nodded with an excited-looking flush under her freckled face. Leading the way and drawing him after her, he waved to Hash that he would be back and let himself be led up the staircase.

In her room, she shut the door and turned to grin big at him.

"I wanted you," she said, gliding over in front of him. "Sit on the bed. I'll pull your boots off."

With expert moves, she soon had him barefoot and pulled him up. She waited for him to undo the gun belt and reach behind her to hang the rig on the straight-back chair. She jerked his belt open like a half-mad prospector going for gold and undid his fly buttons. His britches fell to the floor and her quick hands ran over the outline of his rod under his one-piece underwear.

Unable to contain herself, she undid the button on his one-piece and like a thick spring she unearthed his erection with a deep gush of pleasure coming from her mouth. She dropped to her knees and closed her lips around the head. Taking several inches, she began making *mmm* sounds as she licked and sucked on it like she'd found a new toy. He looked down at the top of her copper-colored head and slowly unbuttoned his shirt. She might be the wildest one he'd had in a while, he thought, recalling the words of the Mexican girl, Elisa, in Socorro who said she never could get over the size of his dick.

Her tongue rasping on the underside, his great erection filled her mouth from corner to corner as she tried to take on more of it. He held her head loosely and his fingers played with her ears, savoring the pleasure that had him on his toes each time she increased her activity. His brain in a swirl, he pulled her up by the arm and she looked disappointed at him but obeyed as they together pulled the duster off over her head.

She wore a snow-white girdle that came to her hips and made her small freckled breasts look ready to pop out of the cups. Wide-eyed and turned on, she pulled him by the arm to get on the bed. On her back, she slithered toward the headboard as he waited for her to get in place with his left knee on the mattress.

A come-hither look on her flushed face, she grinned big and wiped her wet mouth on the back of her hand. A wild gleam of anticipation shone in her green eyes as she stared fixedly at the swinging pendulum under his muscle-corded belly. She spread her legs apart for him to come between them. He noticed the red bush of hair and the small slit below it. When he moved over her, her fingers closed on his hard shaft and she stuck the slick head inside.

At first he pumped easy, opening the way with each push. Like a wild bucking horse, she arched her back off the bed and met his thrusts. The walls of her vagina started to swell with each stroke. Her mouth open, she began to exclaim out loud. "Oh, gawd, that feels so damn good. More, more!"

The ropes under the mattress began to creak and the bed actually moved on the hardwood floor. Slocum stiffened his arms to brace himself and drove his ass harder and harder against her. Then, out of breath and dizzy with desires, the head of his dick began to blossom and he drove it deep inside her—coming in a blinding flood of steam that burned from his testicles until the fiery fluid flew into her.

They collapsed in a pile, half drunk on pleasure's depleting rewards. She pressed her stiff corset hard against him and reached down to fondle his slick tool which made her no mind—though she acted like she couldn't leave it alone. Wind swept through the corner windows, making it cool enough so that Slocum fell asleep.

He awoke with a gun muzzle stuck against his ear. "Don't move mister. My trigger finger is itching to pull this."

4

"Get up easy like. You're under arrest."

"What the hell for?" Slocum saw that the redhead had her duster clutched against her to cover her nakedness and was backed to the wall, looking wide-eyed and fearful.

"For robbing the Lodge Pole, Nebraska, First National Bank."

"When?" Slocum sat on the edge of the bed and combed his fingers through his short hair.

"Ten days ago. We've already got your partner in the heist."

"My partner. Yeah, Micheals."

A realization came to Slocum and he closed his eyes. "Is there a big roan horse hitched at the rack down there?"

"No." the lawman shook his head. "Ain't no roan horse down there. Just them worn-out bays ponies you two boys rode down here."

Slocum focused on the man's snowy mustache that dropped on both sides of his mouth, and the big tin star on his vest. In defeat, he reached for his underwear and the lawman backed up.

"You're looking for Has—Charlie Hash. Stole my roan horse and beat it out of here last night."

"Yeah, sure. Get dressed. We're going back to Nebraska."

"I'm not Hash, I tell you. He obviously stole my roan horse and shagged out of here."

"Well, I'm not the president's nephew either. If I was, I wouldn't be doing this shitty job of chasing down you no-accounts for the county."

Slocum's underwear on, he reached for his pants. The lawman took his money and jackknife out of the pocket, then he handed them over, all the time keeping the six-gun pointed at Slocum and not batting an eye.

"Pay her." Slocum gave a head toss toward the redhead.

"What do you owe her?"

"Twenty bucks."

"Twenty bucks?" The lawman looked taken aback by the price.

"Pay her," Slocum insisted.

"All right." He used his left hand to find the denominations. He tossed them toward the other edge of the bed, where she stood by it, mumbling the whole time that no whore was worth that much.

One hand holding the duster to modestly conceal herself, she came over and snatched them up. The folding money disappeared down the front of her corset and she backed up again.

"Thanks," she said and nodded to Slocum, ignoring the lawman.

"What's your name?" Slocum asked, buttoning his shirt.

"Piper."

"Mr. Piper? Or Piper somebody?"

"Piper."

"Well, Piper, you have the wrong man. Charlie Hash—"

"I don't give a gawdamn about Charlie whoever. I've

got you and Micheals. About a seven-to-ten-year stretch in the Nebraska pen and you two'll be less bank robbers than you were—whoever you are."

"I've never been to Lodge Pole, Nebraska. Ten days ago I was in Sante Fe, New Mexico. I've got an alibi."

"You can tell it to a judge and jury. Stand up." Piper clamped the cuffs on his wrists, slung Slocum's gun holster on his shoulder and pointed toward the door. "Don't try nothing or I'll kill you in a second and save the county the expense of the trial."

"Wait," the redhead shouted and ran over, putting her arm around Slocum's neck. She bent him down to her mouth and kissed him hard. Hard enough, even with his mind filled with desperate ideas of how to escape, so that he recalled their unleashed lovemaking from the night before.

Piper herded him out into the hall and down the stairs. Several round-eyed doves at the base watched him coming toward them. Slocum could see a crestfallen Micheals, also in irons, seated on the sofa, looking at the floor.

Two more deputies armed with shotguns stood ready. One of them looked older with gray whiskers and the other lawman appeared to be so young he hardly had a beard, save a few wild long hairs.

"Get them on their horses," Piper ordered. "And watch them, they look tricky to me."

"Couldn't you lock them up in the woodshed and you boys have a good time with us girls before you leave here?" Irish Rose said, taking charge.

"We like lawmen and would do you guys a big favor," Rose said before they could protest.

"What do you say, Piper?" the kid asked. The crooked smile on his pimply face looked devilish.

"Aw, what can it hurt?" Rose asked, swinging her hips from side to side and marching toward Piper.

"None, I guess, if you all are willing?" The lawman looked them over with a critical eye.

"We're at no cost," Rose said. "You can lock them two in our shed."

"Hell, if you can ever get pussy for free you'd be stupid not to take it," the kid said.

"Earl, go out and look this shed over," Piper said. The gray-bearded one started for the front door to check out the structure.

In minutes he returned. "It'll hold a bull, boss."

"You be damn sure, Earl. I don't aim to chase them down in the Indian Territory," Piper said.

"Well, big man," the redhead said, stepping in and taking the kid's elbow.

"Get over here," Piper said to her and pointed at the toes of his scuffed boots. "I want to try your twenty-dollar stuff."

"Why, of course, darling." She released the kid's arm and came slinking over to the head deputy.

"Got to get them in the shed first," he said, with impatience written all over his tight-skinned face.

"Don't be long," she said, turning and giving him a head to toe once-over across her shoulder. "I'm like candy, I may melt."

Her words brought a nervous titter of laughter from the other women. Those girls had bought Slocum some time. He had worried that Piper might not buy it—the man was no fool. No doubt, from the look of anticipation on the kid's face, he was ready to climb on anyone or all of them. Piper never acted that convinced. As for Earl, he was one apt to be more pleased with a few shots of whiskey than a hop in bed with one of the charming residents. The problem that lay ahead for Slocum was how to get out of the shed and ride the hell away from there.

Marched to the makeshift jail at gunpoint with the door locked outside, Slocum looked at his companion in the light coming from the cracks in the board walls.

"We don't have much time," Micheals said. An unshaven cowboy in his thirties with the hard look of a trapped wolf in his gray eyes, he gave a toss of his stiff dark hair and went over to try to smash off the siding with his boot. After several unsuccessful attempts and nearly losing his balance with his hands cuffed, he cussed aloud. "Those bastards!"

Then both men looked at each other as someone spoke, sticking the end of a lariat through a knothole. It was a dove.

"Here, put this around something in there."

Slocum obeyed her. He threaded the rope out another hole and the person outside drew it tight. He heard the horse milling around, then hooves pounding when it tore out. Boards went to splintering and daylight rushed in, leaving a gaping hole. He saw her on the horse looking back down the rope at the damage to the shed's side. Micheals followed Slocum out into the too bright sunshine.

"Here," a swarthy-skinned girl said, handing Slocum the reins to a stout looking horse. His hat and gun belt were over the horn. He fit the Stetson on his head and said, "Thanks."

With a quick check in the direction of the two-story cathouse, expecting hot lead to come his way any minute, Slocum swung aboard, took the reins in his cuffed hands and had the big sorrel in a hard run across the flats.

Then came the crack of pistol shots from an upstairs window—too late. He and Micheals were chewing up bunch grass and sagebrush with the hard-running ponies between their knees.

"I'll get you . . ." The last threat from the anguished Piper carried on the hard wind in their faces.

They never looked back.

5

Mid-morning they found a small ranch and, feeling they had enough time, rode up to see if there were any black-smithing tools on the place to split the cuff chains.

Piper and his bunch had been left Micheals's and Hash's worn-out ponies to ride. And they also had to catch the mounts, for the girls had sent them running off, Slocum had noticed from the corner of his vision as they left the place. So he and Micheals had time to cut the chains in two, if there were any tools for the job at the place where they'd stopped.

"You see anyone?" Micheals asked, looking around.

Slocum shook his head, halfway expecting someone to show at the house. He milled the sorrel around in a circle, studying the tracks in the dust.

"I think they may have gone to town. See the narrow buggy tracks?"

Micheals nodded and booted his bay to the shed. "Sooner I get out of these damn cuffs the better I'll feel. That no-account Hash has all the damn bank robbery money and that sumbitch left me to rot."

"Both of us," Slocum said, still looking around warily.

"There's tools in here," Micheals said, from the doorway of the toolshed. Slocum saw an anvil and some cold chisels. He nodded in approval, but to hold a chisel and beat on it with his hands together would be hard.

"Put the chain on the end of the anvil. I'll beat the links till they part."

"Guess that's all we can do." Micheals put his hands on both sides and the chain on the surface.

Slocum began to beat a tattoo on the link with a heavy hammer. The metal soon flattened and then parted under his barrage of blows.

Freed to use his hands, Micheals grabbed a chisel and took the hammer. He made four hard hits and Slocum's chain separated. At last he could use his hands. The skin itched under the cuffs but he could live with that. He took a mill file off the bench and nodded to Micheals.

"We better hit the trail."

"Yeah and find that no-account bastard, Hash. I may stake him out on an anthill and put porcupine quills through his balls."

Slocum shook his head at the man's idea of revenge and rushed outside in the sunlight to the red horse. Foot in the stirrup, his first ambition was to shake Piper and his men; then he could worry about taking his ire out on Hash. Though he did owe that no-account for all the trouble he'd caused him.

In the saddle, he looked at the horizon but there was no sign of the posse. With a nod at Micheals, he sent the red horse southward. They avoided cross-country stores and kept off the main road.

"He maybe headed for Sweet Lick," Micheals offered as the hot wind buffed their faces and they rested their horses on a rise in the late afternoon. "What the hell were you doing up there?"

"I had an offer of a job," Slocum said, looking pained, across the sea of waving grass.

"With who?"

"They weren't around when I got there."

Micheals made a scowl of disbelief.

"Yeah, hard to believe, but I never found them anyway."

"I didn't know a soul up there. We were just heading south and stopped off there for what I considered a piece of ass. Damn, I never figured the law was that close to us." He shook his head ruefully and then took off his hat and wiped his forehead with his palm. "That Piper was a tough sumbitch."

"Most bounty men are."

"Sounds like you dealt with them before?"

Slocum agreed without answering him and they reined their horses around and rode on. Using the mill file as they rode, they finally managed to free themselves of the cuffs.

Past dark they reached Lutterell, a small gathering of buildings on a rise. When they rode up the main drag, lamplight from the saloon's front door shone a patch of light out in the street. Checking around, they dismounted and hitched their horses with several others standing hipshot at the rails in the darkness.

"Get some food and a drink. Then we better clear out," Slocum said. "I have a little money in my boot."

"Good," Micheals said as they stopped on the boardwalk adjusting the six-gun on his hip. Slocum fished out his stash of twenty or so dollars and they pushed inside the smoky interior. Slocum in the lead, they sauntered into the barroom.

"What's your pleasure?" the older barkeep asked with a towel in his hand.

"Beer," Slocum said, looking over the crowd in the

smoke-hazy yellow light. Gamblers at two tables, busy with cards in their hands, and some rannies sat at the third one. They looked like ordinary cowboys nursing their beers. One held a saloon girl who appeared to be the center of their attention, on his lap. The only money they had in their pockets no doubt had paid for the beer and she was only tantalizing them in preparation for more prosperous times. Slocum watched her cup both hands under her breasts and raise them up under the blouse so they about shot out of the low-cut front. From their loud responses, she had stirred something up with them.

Micheals downed his brew and headed for the lunch counter.

"Traveling through?" the barkeep asked Slocum, making small talk as he polished a stein.

"Yeah, how far is the line?"

"Half a day's ride."

"Them big cattle outfits in the Cherokee Strip hiring down there?" Slocum asked, making conversation.

"You know you can't own a brand and work for them?" The bartender had a warning in his look.

"I'd heard they did that."

"Them rich bastards want all the gravy."

Slocum agreed, gave a head toss toward the food to excuse himself and went to join Micheals.

"We better eat and ride, huh?" Micheals said under his breath, between bites on a hard-boiled egg.

Slocum agreed.

Ten minutes later, they were headed south under the stars. His stomach not churning on emptiness any longer and more relaxed now, Slocum rode loose in the saddle. Piper would keep coming. He knew the kind. Somewhere he needed to split from Micheals. Two were easier to track than one anyway. Secondly, despite his traveling pard's show of evenness, Slocum felt a sleeping giant was caged inside the man.

Close to dawn they rested their horses at a tank and windmill. Taking a short catnap, Slocum awoke with the sun's golden spears in his swollen sore eyes. He rose, stiff from the long haul, and used his hands to wash his face in the tepid water. The baptism did little to awaken him more. With his kerchief he dried off and tried to focus through the golden brilliance on the northern horizon for signs of pursuit—nothing.

"Where do you reckon that worthless Hash is right now?" Micheals asked in a sleep-frogged voice.

"Hard to say."

"It damn sure ain't hard for me to say. I'll kill the sumbitch when I get him." Micheals cut a hocker out of his throat and spat it in the dust.

Slocum caught up his sorrel and tightened the cinch. "We might lose them when we get over into the Cherokee Strip."

Micheals looked north with squinted eyes. "I hope so."

His toe in the stirrup, Slocum knew in his heart that men like Piper never gave up. Like the hounds of hell, they kept on and on—until they found their quarry or someone killed them.

Bar City sat astraddle the line between Kansas and the Strip. They reached there in mid-afternoon. The bars were on the Kansas side, since whiskey was prohibited in the Strip. From what Slocum had heard, the Kansas legislature planned to dry up that state too. Be tough for a man to get a glass of anything before long.

The hoot of a steam engine made the sorrel about spook out from under him despite his weariness.

Micheals looked amused and laughed. "Old sorrel about dumped you."

"Close. Say, I've got eighteen dollars left. That's nine apiece. What say we split up here. Two trails are harder to follow than one."

Micheals batted his eyelashes in disbelief. "You mean you'd give me half the last money you got?"

"Why not?"

He took off his hat, used his palm to wipe his sweaty forehead and then shook his head. "Can't believe it. I'll sure take it, but I ain't so sure I'd ever be that generous when I was down to my last twenty."

Slocum handed him the folding money and Micheals stuck it in his vest pocket. "I owe you. I figured that if you hadn't been so generous with that whore—that twenty buck deal—we'd both be in a Nebraska jail. I damn sure wasn't with mine. I paid mine six bits; course she didn't know I had all that bank money either, at the time. She thought I was some out of work hand and using my last quarters on her."

Slocum stuck out his hand then quickly caught the reins as the red horse shied at yet another train whistle coming from the cattle yards. They shared a grin and Micheals rode off to the west of the town; Slocum rode up the main street.

He put the sorrel in the livery and paid six bits for a rub-down, grain and hay. Then he went across the street to the two-story White House Hotel, checked in and after discussing a hot bath with the clerk went up to his room. The bath was supposed to be ready in ten minutes in the facilities at the end of the hall. Some Chinaman would clean and press his clothes. He could wear a robe they provided their customers with back to his room while his laundry was being done.

A half hour later, lying on top of the bed, he heard a knock on the door. Half asleep, he rolled off the bed onto his bare feet and his hand was filled with the Colt from the lawman's saddlebags.

"Yes?"

"Slocum?" It was a woman's voice.

6

When Slocum opened the door, he blinked his eyes as the woman dressed in a blue dress with a shawl over her head swept past him. She looked familiar. He closed the door, after first checking to be sure that she was alone in the hallway. Setting her carpetbag down, she pulled free the shawl.

"I'm Judy Steward," she said, out of breath. "I lied to the clerk and said I was your wife."

"How in the hell did you get here?"

"You weren't hard to track."

"You see any sign of them lawmen coming this way?"

She shook her head as she raised her face and combed the blond hair back with her fingers. "They were still looking for horses to buy when I left Bender's Gap. The selection at the local livery was poor. I doubt they found any suitable mounts for several days."

"You're serious?" he asked, looking hard at her attractive face. The slender nose and high cheekbones gave her tanned face a delicate look but the blue eyes under web-thick lashes could burn a hole through a man or warm his

37

heart—whichever she chose to do at the moment. The bridgework of her breasts under the frilly lace on the front of her dress looked proud. Her slender waist appeared just right to hold in both hands and draw her to him—but he chose to refrain from that until he knew more about her purpose in being there.

"You're the J. Steward?" He shook his head, amazed at his own discovery and why he'd never guessed it before.

"Yes, my father is a tyrant and I needed to be free of him before I could approach you."

"You're free now?"

"Oh, no. Your getting arrested and escaping messed up everything." She looked at the ceiling's tin squares for help.

"I never robbed that Nebraska Bank." He showed her the bed to sit upon, then he drew up the straight-back chair to straddle and face her.

"I figured that out. But also, Rose told me some guy named Hash had stolen your horse and left you to face the law."

"That's that. Why do you need me?"

"My brother Steven is an impulsive gambler and has lost lots of money that he doesn't have the means to pay back. My father has refused to pay his ransom and some thugs will kill him if I can't save him."

"Who and where are they?"

"They're in Deadwood. The one's name is Jake Hamilton and the other is Farris Cunningham."

"Deadwood's a tough place. We'd have to get on the Union Pacific in Nebraska to get to Cheyenne and take the Black Hills Stage Line up to Deadwood. The stage trip alone takes four days and we're a week away from the train up there, plus the time to get to Cheyenne."

"I know we may get there too late, but he's my brother and I'd like to save him."

"I'm broke. Law got what little money I had up there."

"I have enough money. Not the thousands that they're demanding but I have some money."

"You are talking about fresh horses for both of us and it may take more. We ride that hard, we'll use up several. Then train and stage tickets. Lodging and food, then we may need to put up a front up there."

"Did I say I had enough money?" She looked, perturbed, at him.

"Fine, but enough?"

"Enough—I can pay you as well—and I understand the situation is tight. I'll pay you even if we can't save poor Steven."

A smile crept into the corners of his mouth over the prospects of such an arrangement. "This Mrs. role might get out of control."

"I can handle that." She began unbuttoning her dress down the front. "You may as well see your new wife in the buff. Fair enough?"

He nodded and wet his lips in anticipation of the viewing of his "wife."

"Well—I am not undressing by myself, Mr. Slocum." Her busy finger paused and she looked up and met his gaze. "Sauce for the gander, sauce for the goose."

"Drive on," he said and rose astraddle the chair and undid the robe's belt.

Soon she began shrugging out of her dress top, then laid the garment aside. He watched her firm breasts quake under the shimmering camisole. Seated on the bed, she began to unroll her stockings and revealed her slender legs.

He had never really considered her height before. Hardly much over four foot eight or nine—like dynamite, she came in a small package. Strange, he had thought her to be much taller all along, but as she undressed he realized her petite size.

Removing the robe and placing it on the chair's back, he turned and studied her cute bare butt—a long, drawn-out one that sloped like a bannister's curve. She was fast taking his breath away.

Then a frontal view of her hugging the pear-shaped breasts made his erection stiffen harder. Obviously she was taken aback by the sight and size of his dusty pink shaft for she looked hard at it, then shook her head as if in disbelief. "Whew."

He straightened and smiled reassuringly at her. "He's not half as bad as he looks."

With a wary shake of her head, tossing her shoulder-length hair back, she stepped forward and he took her in his arms. His stiff rod folded against her firm stomach as he bent over and kissed her. Her arms flew around his neck and their mouths turned to fire.

With his right hand, he weighed her left breast and he smiled with pleasure as they kissed harder. What a body. She pulled him toward the bed.

With her gaze locked upon him, she crawfished on her back to the center, the light-colored bush triangle exposed as she spread her snowy legs apart and rolled her shoulders in anticipation. He climbed on the bed and half atop of her, and bent over to savor the pointed left nipple.

She cried out when his lips closed on the rock-hard tip and his tongue began to tease her. Her hand groped for his shaft and when she found it she gently ran the skin back and forth over the turgid muscles. Then her fingers cupped the rock-hard head of his dick and she gasped.

Squirming downward she sought to put him away. Slocum raised up and obliged her. Easing the head into her moist tunnel, she closed her eyes in anticipation and threw her head back, exposing the oval chiseled chin.

"Oh, dear God—" escaped her lips as he drove the hard-on home.

The swollen dick tightly filled her cunt and she caught her breath when he struck the bottom. But she arched her back for all of it and closed her lashes. Her rose-petal bottom lip fell open, exposing her straight teeth, and she began to moan. The bed ropes creaked in protest and Slocum was enjoying each stroke. Her butt raised up off the mattress in wild abandonment to meet his thrusts and he felt her begin to swell inside.

Then she collapsed in a faint and he was forced to pause his fight. Bleary-eyed she began to regain her senses.

"Lord, what else—"

"Hold tight, we've just got started," he said and laughed softly when she looked up at him bug-eyed then smiled when his actions began to move her back toward passion's door.

They were both soon in wild flight, grunting, stressing, straining and using every effort to reach a peak from each other. The head of his dick felt loaded to the hilt with cannon powder. When the charge was ignited, a mule kicked him in both testicles, two Indian lances struck him in the buttocks and he exploded inside her.

They both fell into a calm embrace. Her body curled against him and his chin rested on the top of her head. He closed his eyes and slept.

In the late afternoon, with her advance of money, he went to the livery, traded in the sorrel and her bay and bought three fresh horses and a pack saddle. Then he went across to the general store, purchased two bedrolls, a few pots and pans, tin plates and cups, some flour, rice, dried beans, crackers, dry cheese, bacon, baking powder, air-tight tomatoes, canned peaches, sugar and coffee. With all his supplies loaded in the panniers and a new holster for the .45, he led the horses across the street and hitched them at the rack in front of the hotel.

Judy came down from the room wearing men's canvas pants, suspenders and a man's shirt. With her hair swept up under a broad-brimmed straw hat, except for her breasts she looked like a boy. She stepped aboard the light-stepping bay he had bought for her and they headed north-west in the copper sunset's glow. He rode a darker blood bay and the brown pack horse led easy.

His plan to leave both their horses might make Piper think they'd taken a stage, especially if he knew she was with him. Either way, with a good head start they would be in Nebraska in a week. Then they'd take the train to Cheyenne and the stage to Deadwood. If Piper ever sorted out all the twists and turns, he was a better man than most.

They rode till past midnight, then with a coyote sere-nade they slept in one bedroll till dawn. Up and in the sad-dle in a few minutes and sharing a can of sweet peaches passed back and forth, they steered themselves far enough west so no one would recognize her.

"You ever been married?" Slocum asked her.

She wet her lips, turned her look off as if to follow the flight of a meadowlark. "Are you asking where did I learn about men?"

"Yeah."

"No boy was ever good enough for me," she said. "My father wanted me to go to finishing school. Marry some rich guy from the east. I had other plans.

"The first guy in my bed was a cowboy, of course." She wrinkled her nose and shook her head. "He got it halfway in me and came.

"My, I thought that was great fun. Then he swallowed and got red-faced, jerked up his pants and ran away. I just figured that's what men did to women."

They both laughed and Slocum discarded the empty tin.

"Martin Tyler came in my life next. He was a suave kind of guy. Rode for some of the other outfits like the ZKT. A year or two older than Dewey, my first lover, and Tyler'd been around. We took to meeting at water tanks. We went swimming in our clothes at first. Before long we went swimming without our clothes so we didn't have to wait for them to dry. He had a little stinger, even smaller than Dewey's. But he knew how to use it."

She made a face. "Gave me a big scare. Thought he had me in a family way. But he didn't.

"I went to see Rose then and made friends with her."

"Rose have something for that?"

"Yes, it's worked so far. Meanwhile Tyler got all hot and bothered by a Polish girl over at Norwin. I knew he was seeing her too, but I kinda liked him anyway. Well, he really got her in a family way and her father and brothers gave him a shotgun option. Marry her or die.

"Then there was Luke. He worked for my father. Nice-looking guy about your size. He caught me one morning in the barn, bent over gathering some eggs in the hay. In a split second he whipped up my dress, jerked down my bloomers and had his thing throbbing hard up between my legs.

"What could I do? I reached down and put him inside. He shouted so loud at me doing that I thought he'd wake the dead or bring paw to the barn on the run. His hands cradling my hips, he gave me what for from behind, then at the last minute jerked it out and came all over my legs.

"Guess he figured that would save him having to marry me."

"You and him do it again?" Slocum asked, pointing toward a wagon track ahead he planned for them to use.

"Oh yeah, in the cellar, in the hay, on the porch swing with me in his lap. No nerve, he wouldn't try to sneak in the house and do it upstairs in my bed. There were two other cowboys in the bunkhouse so that was out. I guess you were my first time to get it in a real bed."

"Good. We better lope awhile if we're ever going to get to Nebraska."

"Yes," she agreed and looked back over her shoulder. He followed suit and saw nothing but waving grass. Good—they had a long ways to go.

7

Five days later he sold the horses and gear to a livery in Powder, Nebraska. Then he bought a suit in a haberdashery and she got out her blue dress. The man tailored the clothes for Slocum that afternoon and he wore the new ones when they climbed on the 8:10 a.m. westbound. Under the alias of Mr. and Mrs. Sutherland with tickets for Salt Lake City to throw off any pursuit—they would be in Cheyenne in twelve hours. They sat in their hard seats and watched the Platte Valley rush by. A constant song of the clacks of the rail joints underneath them, Slocum recalled the sorrel's first response when the engineer hit the whistle. The side-to-side sway of the car making her nod her head enough to curl under his arm and sleep.

The nighttime temperature was cool enough that she got out her shawl on the platform in Cheyenne. He herded her, half asleep, to a taxi and the hotel. In minutes she was asleep on the bed and he quietly left the room and went down to the hotel bar.

"How things going up at Deadwood?" he asked the bartender over his beer.

45

"Ask Wayne. He just came back from there."

Wayne, a big man with stooped shoulders, turned, shifted to his other elbow and looked introspectively at Slocum. "You heading up there?"

"Planned to. How tough is it?"

"Still plenty of Sioux war parties roaming around between here and there. They ain't happy either."

"I've heard that."

"A bunch of them red niggers struck us, but we had enough fire power." The man shook his head in disapproval. "Not to mention the stage robbers. They rob that stage about once a week. Know when there's something or someone valuable on it. Like they've got spies. What's your business up there?"

"Thought I'd go see it."

"Well it ain't much of a tourist stopover. More like hell. Mister, it's like all the rest of them mining towns. Restless, ruthless and full of whores."

"Mine's business."

After another glass of beer, he went back to their room, undressed and climbed in bed to curl around her. Half awake, she reached back and grasped his shaft. In a few minutes, he had her up on her knees, his legs spread apart to fit her and pouring the meat to her from behind—her *ooh's* and *ah's* loud enough to let the other hotel tenants know that they were making real love, her tight walls causing enough friction to make his brains boil until he finally came and collapsed in a pile on top of her.

Maybe if the Indians were acting that tough, she should stay in Cheyenne. He'd hate for anything to happen to her. But she'd never accept that—she was going to Deadwood to try to rescue her brother.

He felt her small fingers wrapped around his dick for safe-keeping as he fell asleep.

• • •

The first available tickets he could buy for their departure were for the Tuesday stage—that meant a two-day lay-over. He was on the boardwalk headed back for the hotel when he spotted a familiar figure among the busy street traffic—Hash.

How had he gotten up there? Good question. Slocum felt for the Colt under his suit coat and then began to walk faster to keep in sight of the weather-beaten cowboy hat. The bank-robber Hash had not gone south when he left with Slocum's roan and the loot as his partner had expected. Made sense. Slocum excused himself for half colliding with a lady on the boardwalk.

Then Hash turned up a side street and Slocum hurried to see where he had gone. But by the time he crossed through the traffic, with many delays going around passing vehicles, his quarry was not in sight. That the outlaw no longer rode his roan was one thing he was certain about. How much of the bank loot was left was the second question. Knowing how most outlaws spent their ill-gotten gains, Slocum figured that Hash was probably close to broke by this time.

Once, in Denver, Slocum had been in a den of iniquity when two Wyoming road agents hit town with the proceeds of a large robbery, listed in the papers as amounting to over ten thousand dollars. The two were hardly more than boys who had left cowpunching for a higher paying occupation.

They arrived liquored up at Madam Duprey's and promptly began to screw every whore in her stable. The two's stamina outmatched the likes of any known studs. In their rush of generosity, they ordered a barrel of fresh oysters at twelve dollars a pound, six crates of French champagne, and enough prime rib to feed an army. They refused to let any of the other guests pay for anything and the party lasted five days.

The youngest of the pair, Billy Rand, was stark naked, doing it doggy-style to a house girl called Phoebe in the middle of the living room. He was fanning her with his cowboy hat like a bronc rider when the Pinkerton men rushed in and arrested them.

No money was recovered. The boys got ten years apiece in the Wyoming Territorial pen for their part. Both were pardoned in less than five—but, Slocum figured as he hurried toward the hotel, they must have told the story of their wild party over and over again.

"What do you mean Hash is here?" Judy asked, dressed in a thin duster.

"Micheals's partner that stole my horse and left me to take his place is here in Cheyenne."

"What are you going to do about it?"

"If he has any of the money left, I'm going to charge him for my inconvenience."

She wrinkled her nose. "I have money. Don't risk anything. I want to get to Deadwood and find Steven and hope that he is alive." She moved in front of him and fussed with his tie as if improving his dress.

"Stage is booked full. We can't leave until Tuesday."

"Can't we ride up there faster than that?"

"No. Too dangerous. The Sioux are on the war path all over that country and there's lots of war parties. We'd make fine easy bait for them. The stagecoach is the only safe way."

She moved in closer, looked up at him and then smiled as her hand slid over the mound under his fly. "Oh, what can we do?"

His head thrown back, Slocum laughed aloud. Then he crushed her against his body. "You'd sure wear out two good men."

"I ain't worn you out yet."

He closed his eyes and toed off his boots. Not yet.

After dark, Slocum dressed in his cowboy gear and left Judy in the room. At their meal taken earlier in the hotel restaurant, Slocum thought he saw someone else he knew— Cranston Bleiu, a gambler originally from Louisiana; he'd known him in south Texas from a few years before. Neither man had given any sign of recognition to the other and so the matter lay ahead as to whether Cranston even wanted anyone to know him from before or not.

A short while later, Slocum slipped inside the smoky interior of the first bar. The sounds of tinkling glass and the free laughter of doves filled his ears, while the sour smell of booze and chewing tobacco soon filled his nostrils. He ordered a beer at the bar and then let his eyes adjust to the candle-powered lighting.

There were several gambling on the wheel and others sat at side tables considering their poker hands. Some professor was tickling the ivories on a tinny piano and another mustached hombre under a derby was seated on a high stool and plunking on a "bug"—some form of small mandolin.

"You come up with a herd?" the guy beside him asked.

Slocum shook his head to the man. "Came looking is all."

"You looking for me?" the dark-eyed girl asked, stalking over to him.

"Might be," Slocum said as she joined him. He gave a head toss to the barkeep to bring her a drink.

"What you looking for?" she said, eyeing him from head to toe.

"An old pal named Hash."

"Corned beef?" she teased, running her index finger familiarly under his suspender strap.

"No. Just another ranny."

"I don't know him, but I find him, I'll tell him you're here."

Slocum shook his head. "Save it for a surprise."

"I will. Thanks for the drink. You want some real pussy, you ask for Candy, I sleep right out back." She gave a toss of her short black hair toward the rear of the place.

The Roaring Bull Moose and the other saloons he checked had no knowledge of Hash, at least, not by that name. From what he had learned so far, Charlie Hash had not tried to use his bank loot to set the lights up in one of the local whorehouses and drawn attention to his philanthropy. It was a typical way most robbers were caught—they flashed the cash and had a party.

With nothing else to go on, Slocum pushed his way out into the night and started for the first livery.

"Wait, mister."

Slocum turned and saw a crippled man with a stiff leg coming up the dark boardwalk. When he entered the ring of light from the lamppost, Slocum could see he looked harmless enough.

"I know where this guy Hash is," the man said in a whiskey-flavored breath. Then he looked around to be certain he would not be overheard. "You willing to pay a little for the info?"

"How much?"

"How much is he worth?"

"Probably not much."

The man held out his hand. "Put some silver in me palm and I'll tell you."

Slocum obliged him.

"He's staying up at Myrtle Brown's sheep camp. She ain't half bad to look at. Got big tits and she's soft on him."

"Where's she at?"

"Up on the road north to Casper. Somewhere this side of Chugwater—"

"Thanks." In the morning he'd rent a horse and go find Myrtle Brown's camp. Hash might have enough money left to pay him for the roan horse, anyway. Slocum watched the man limp off back toward the bar. His change should buy him a few more drinks at least.

Back in the hotel room, Judy reared up in the bed, clutching the sheet to her and smiling at him when he came in. The soft lamplight danced on her snowy bare shoulder and she gave a toss of her hair.

"Learn anything?"

"Yeah, he's herding sheep." He toed off his boots.

"Why's that?" She wrinkled her nose in distaste.

"Oh, there is a woman involved I guess. She owns the sheep."

"You still going looking for him?"

He hung his gun belt on the straight chair back. "Not tonight."

"Good," she said, sounding pleased, and snuggled back into the bed. The sheet pulled up to her chin, she looked up at the tin ceiling squares. "I had other plans for you."

8

The green sheep-wagon with a sun-yellow canvas top sat on a rise above the low-roofed scramble of buildings used for lambing. The sheds, some with sod roofs low enough that one would have to stay bent over to be inside of them, were tucked under the brow of the hill so the north wind would sweep over them.

A couple of ring-neck collies came barking at Slocum's approach. Then someone in a green shirt, too short a person to be Hash, came out of the wagon. As Slocum drew closer he saw that she filled out the blouse with her amble bustline, like the man said.

"Morning, Myrtle Brown," he said, setting the horse and letting the cool wind sweep his face.

She squinted her green eyes at him and used one hand to shade them. "Guess we ain't properly met."

"Properly, I'm Slocum. Looking for Hash. He here?"

She wrinkled her nose and shook her head. The thick braid hung over her shoulder. "He left the day before."

"Guess he never said where he would light next."

"Climb down. I've got coffee and we can talk about our mutual friend, Hash."

"Well, I ain't the law." He hesitated dismounting to wait for her reply.

"Hell, I know all them Wyoming lawmen. Knew you wasn't law when you rode in. Get down, unless you're afraid of me." She studied him for a second from head to toe. "You ain't half bad looking."

Then she hiked up her many skirts and went up the back steps.

Inside the wagon, the translucent light coming through the material cast a yellowish glow over the interior. She indicated a chair and poured him coffee in a metal cup. Then she set the last piece of apple pie in the tin before him.

Slocum nodded in approval at her hospitality. He'd left Cheyenne long before daylight with no breakfast. He accepted her fork. The trailer held the musk of a woman, along with the aroma of wood smoke and spices. The front portion was taken up with a great feather bed. Behind it was a tidy, small space with an iron cook/heating stove, a small dry sink and cabinets all around.

The pie drew the saliva in his mouth and the rich coffee drove the morning cobwebs from his mind.

"What're you after Hash for?"

"He still riding a roan horse?"

"Yeah, got a cross bar on him."

"That's my horse. He left me a run-in-the-ground mustang in the roan's place and a lawman after that horse's rider who stuck a gun in my face."

She laughed out loud and slapped her knee. "That Hash is a cutter. I wondered what kinda trouble he was into this time."

"He say where he was going?"

"Deadwood, I guess."

Slocum nodded. He'd meet up with him there.

"I'm obliged, and for the pie too," he said.

"Shame you rode plumb out here for nothing."

"Oh, I'd hardly say nothing."

"I was thinking I might ought to make it worth your time."

"Oh."

She stood up and began to unbutton the green blouse. "Well down your coffee and get undressed. I always can tell by the look in his eyes when a man wants some."

He finished the coffee and smiled. "I'd be obliged, ma'am."

She threw back her head and laughed aloud. "Obliged indeed." Her melon-sized breasts capped with brown russets quaked as she untied the waist of her many layered skirts. "Guess I'll have to be grateful that Hash stopped off here." Her laughter sounded free, not haughty nor mocking—it had an openess. When he was undressed he gave a head toss for him to get up there and shoved him up into the bed with a hand on his butt.

The feather bed acted like a wavy ocean and they bounced like they were on clouds getting on top of it. He glanced over at her on her hands and knees beside him. Plenty of flesh there; she wasn't tall and her bare legs looked even shorter than they had.

With a flip of the braid, she lay on her side and looked at him with her sleepy green eyes, smiling at him when his free hand fondled her rock-hard nipples. With effort they moved closer and he tasted her mouth while her groping fingers squeezed his half-hard manhood. Consumed with an obvious flash of fire, she closed her eyes and scooted closer to him.

"I can't wait any longer." She drew her knees up and

guided him between them. He clamored about on the spongy bed-top like a sailor on the deck of a swaying ship.

When he dropped down, she smiled, pleased, and raised her butt for his entry. He poked him into her wet gates and she sighed, pulling him down on top of her bridgework. With each thrust he grew harder and bigger. The walls of her vagina began to swell and soon she was moaning and straining hard. For a moment she went limb with her own pleasure, then she recovered sleepy-eyed, and began again to reach for the height of his hard punching.

He counted four orgasms for her by the time his fury really began to build. Over him, the trailer's canopy was shaking from their efforts. He drove his ass hard into her each time, and spasms in the walls of her cunt grasped his dick so tightly they made his efforts to push back in more strenuous with each stroke.

His breathing raged and the sweat streaked off his body. When the head on his dick felt ready to explode he reached down with both hands, gripped her rock-hard ass, and drove him home as deep as he could. Then he strained and the depleting round fired inside, which made her clutch him and cry out. Finally, her heels beating a tattoo on his butt, they collapsed in a pile.

"You gong to Deadwood too?" she asked in a hoarse whisper.

"Tomorrow."

"Figured so." She nodded and smiled. "You ever get lost up this way again, stop in."

"I will. He say what he was going to do up there?"

She shook her head and twisted the braid in her hand. "Knowing him—he'll probably blow all his money and be back here broke again."

"You'll take him in?"

"Hell, I'm a sucker for a big dick and a grinning cow-boy." She shook her head in dismay. "Look at you."

With his fist he raised her chin, leaned over and kissed her. "No, you're quite a lady, Myrtle Brown. I'll try to drop by again some day."

She scooted on her butt across the feather bed to get to edge. "I believe you will."

Past dark, he made it back to Cheyenne and the livery. The stable boy took his rental horse and led him off down the dimly lit row of tie stalls filled with horses. Slocum put the saddle and pads on the first empty rack on the wall. He left the horse-sweat-smelling office and headed for the ho-tel down the under-lit street. He planned to settle with Hash in Deadwood when he arrived there, and hoped they weren't too late to save Judy's brother.

He knocked on the hotel room door and he heard her say, "Coming."

The door came open and she looked relieved. "I was worried. Did you find him?"

"No, he rode on to Deadwood. Had supper?"

She put her face on his vest. "I thought you might've had trouble."

"Why?" he said, hugging her. "Have you eaten?"

"No, have you?"

"No." Not since this piece of pie earlier in the day.

"I'll brush my hair," she said.

"Fine."

"I read in the newspaper today that they had arrested one of the men—a Franklin Micheals, who robbed the Lodge Pole, Nebraska Bank." She stopped brushing, wait-ing for his reply.

"Where did they get him?"

"Said in Kansas."

Slocum nodded. A good thing they'd lit a shuck for Cheyenne. Piper was a tough lawman, he wouldn't quit easy. Maybe by this time Micheals had told him Hash was his real partner. He could hope for a lot. Better yet, he'd be glad to be on the Deadwood stage in the morning and on the move again.

"Ready," she said and smiled as she swept by him through the door he held open.

He drew in a deep breath for strength. She'd expect him to be up for her too later. Whew!

9

They crossed the purplish-tinged sagebrush sea, leaving boiling dust in their wake. The coach rocked from front to back and the eight occupants were tucked inside like sardines in a Norwegian tin without the oil to lubricate them. Slocum and Judy shared the front bench with a drummer, a short man who wore a derby hat and a cheap, rumpled suit, who looked hungover—a situation he obviously was treating with more of the hair of the dog, for his breath reeked of whiskey. Two women sat in the center seat, both of such ample proportions that the man supposed to sit there with them chose the top. In the rear, three men sat in a haughty fashion. One had a sharp-pointed beard and gold-rimmed glasses. The man on his right wore the hard look of an ex-con and the man on his left, another drummer, was red-faced and already mopping his sweaty brow with a kerchief, despite the morning's coolness.

"Ever been to Deadwood before?" the man on the other side of Judy asked them.

She shook her head and tried to scoot closer to

Slocum—obviously she was wedged so tightly against the drummer it was making her feel uncomfortable.

"How about you, sir?"

Slocum shook his head.

"They say it is the next San Francisco."

"Without a railroad or seaport I doubt it," Slocum said, watching a badger stand on his hind legs at some distance from the road, then whirl and disappear.

"They're building a railroad to there."

"Good."

"You know how to mine for gold?"

"I've panned a little," Slocum offered. "But I can tell you right now, the big finds have been made up there and they are owned already by powerful people. All that's left is a few flecks of dust in the creeks."

"The peelings," the drummer said and nodded in solemn agreement. Then he took a pint out of his pocket and offered it to Slocum, who shook his head. The man took a swallow. "It's for my stomach."

Neither of the dowagers approved and looked aghast at the man's performance.

"Devil rum, sir," the gray-headed woman said.

"No, ma'am, rye whiskey."

"The same. It should be prohibited from trade."

Her partner accordioned her three chins in agreement. "The vile stuff should never be sold."

"I can see we have some disagreement here," the man with the pointed beard joined in.

"If you intend to defend alcoholic consumption—"

"Hardly, my dear woman, but it has its place to numb pain both physical and mental."

"Numb pain! It turns men into monsters, deprives children of substance and makes slaves of the drinkers' mates."

Slocum slumped down, satisfied his knees would miss

the second woman's, who looked bursting to join in the de-liberation. He intended to get some sleep.

They reached the first relay stopover and the driver let them out to vent their bladders and stretch their legs. A white-bearded man in a leather shirt and wide-brimmed hat, the driver, Clell, drawled like a Texan and spat tobacco with an accuracy that the open-coach passengers should have been grateful for. The burly shotgun guard who talked with a Scandinavian accent spoke to the Professor, Slocum's title for the pointed-beard man.

"We won't have no Injun trouble till we get past Fort Laramie," the guard told the Professor.

"Good. How serious is the trouble up there?"

"Well, it ain't no Sunday school picnic. Dem Injuns are mad as hornets over losing them hills and they take it out on anything a white man has."

"The government paid them well for the land, I under-stand."

"Dat ain't the problem. They didn't want to sell it."

"They don't understand."

"Yeah, dat's it." The guard lumbered off to use the facil-ities out back.

"Will we have Indian trouble?" Judy asked Slocum.

"No telling, the Sioux are pretty vindictive about the loss of the hills."

"Can a stage hold out?"

"There are stages all the time going in and out. The Army is guarding the road. Not every inch, but they're out after the hostiles. We may not see a thing of them."

"I hope not. I just want to find Steven alive and get him out of there."

Slocum nodded. "We're going to try."

They reached Fort Laramie close to sunset, rumbled over the iron bridge and halted at the log station. Every bone in Slocum's body ached when he climbed off and helped Judy down.

"This may be the best meal stop," he said under his breath.

"I don't know if I can eat and keep it down."

"You better eat something. You'll get weak. The rest of the stops are way stations and the food at them will be much worse."

She looked at him hard, the golden-red of the sundown reflecting off of her hard-set face. "We still have two and a half more days of this?"

"We're just getting started."

The coach rumbled across the moonlit sagebrush sea, stopping at relay points to change horses and then go on. The snores of men and an occasional loud fart over the horses' hooves pounding the ground, harness jingle, leather strain, were all heard, as well as the latest driver Jim's shouts and the iron rims cutting the gritty surface.

The passengers, all hungover and dust-floured, blinked in disbelief at the dawn trying to ease itself over the wide eastern horizon. They stood numb, half awake, before the sod house that Jim said would serve breakfast inside. Slocum returned with Judy from the fly infested outhouses in the back and they washed their hands on the porch after the others. The filthy rags used for towels made the effort seem useless but they shrugged and went inside.

An Indian woman served bowls of what looked like oatmeal, and coffee in chipped cups.

"No sweetener?" the number one dowager asked the shabbily dressed server.

The Indian woman shook her head slightly as if she had heard that complaint before and could do nothing about it.

Slocum wiped his spoon on his pants until it shone and then nodded to Judy. No need to complain, the food would get worse before they reached Deadwood, he felt certain. They both ate without words.

The wind switched out of the south and the passenger compartment was filled with the wake dust whenever the driver drew down. At first the two dowagers, Mrs. Green, the oldest, and Mrs. Blaine, the other, fought the brown cloud with their hands. But the futility of that soon proved itself and they, like the rest, endured it—although the wrinkles in their necks soon became seams of dirt, while the color of their new blue dresses turned an ash-like shade.

Wimbleton ran out of his carefully rationed whiskey in the middle of day two and that left him to fidget. The tough guy rode on top. He had traded places with the youth, who obviously had not slept any the night before from fear of falling off his perch. He slept blissfully in the corner.

They were crossing a high point marked with some jack pines. The horses were in a long walk when Slocum turned his ear to the coyote cries. Indians.

He could see them, barreling down off the ridge. Maybe two dozen, redskins on painted ponies. No mistaking them; they wanted blood. He felt Judy clasp his arm and suck in her breath.

"Oh! Dear God!" Mrs. Green gasped.

Shouting at the top of his lungs, Jim threw the reins to the horses and the coach lurched about on the leather straps. Slocum managed to unbuckle his gun belt and pull it out. He handed it to her and indicated for her to push some cartridges out of the loops. Pale-faced, she obeyed, but her fingers trembled.

"Don't you have a gun?" Mrs. Green demanded of Wimbleton.

"No, ma'am, and I ain't got any whiskey left either.

The yapping attackers were closing in. Slocum heard the Swede give the big man on top a rifle and told him to hold his fire. The wide-eyed youth bolted up and his face blanched white at the impending situation.

"What'll we do?" he asked.

"Fight them. Change places," the Professor said, brandishing a long-barreled Colt. The weapon, an obvious changeover from black powder, looked useable enough. Next, the pop of shots began to fill the air, mixed with screams and horses lunging faster as the war-painted Indians on buffalo ponies drew closer.

Soon the lead rider, with a scowl on his red-and-yellow-streaked face drew up beside the coach, a rifle held ready. He looked down the barrel of Slocum's handgun. The six-gun spoke in his hand and the rider threw his hands up, hit hard in the chest.

"You got him!" Mrs. Blaine shouted.

The Professor shot twice. The rifle above them fired, then the roar of the Swede's shotgun's double blast made the yipping stop and the attackers veered away into the sage and bunch grass.

"We've whipped them," Mrs. Green shouted.

"Don't count on it, madam," the Professor said. "We have only begun to fight."

"We're going to make the ridge," Jim shouted. "But they've hit the big guy up here."

Slocum wondered why the man had only fired the rifle once. Obviously he had received his answer. He punched the casing out and reloaded.

"There's a ranch a few miles up the road," Jim shouted to them. "I'll try to make it."

Slocum shed his hat in Judy's lap and stuck himself out the window to look for the war party. He could see them behind the funnel of dust; no doubt they were counting their dead and working up more courage to attack again. The Indian he shot might have been the party's leader. The buck's true value to them was something worth speculating over, anyway, when they were grasping at straws for survival.

Half an hour later Slocum saw the column of smoke streaking the sky ahead. Before anyone asked, he knew the answer. Their hopes for some place of safety had been set ablaze, no doubt after a bloody raid. He knew what a burning homestead looked like when it streaked the azure sky.

"What's wrong?" Judy asked softly when he sat back in the seat.

"There's no ranch left."

She nodded to show she heard him and the two sisters' faces blanched white.

"What will we do?"

"Turn into empty whiskey bottles and lay beside the road," Wimbleton said in disgust. "Nobody would want us then."

"Let us pray," Mrs. Green said and without any consensus began to speak to the Lord. Her request proved quite lengthy but everyone endured her devotional and said "Amen" at the end with her.

Slocum took off his hat again to look out but could see nothing in their dusty wake.

"How far is the next station?" he shouted to Jim.

"About six or seven miles."

"Can you see them back there?"

"No," the Swede answered him.

He slumped back inside. They were still a good ways from the next change of horses and any help, and the bucks had not given up. In fact, the war party would surely come fiercer the next time, since they had lost some of their own.

With no idea how defensible the next station was, they rolled past the burned-out ranch.

"Don't look!" Slocum shouted to the others as the acrid smoke of the blackened framework swept inside the cab.

Four naked mutilated bodies lay on the ground as if set out for all to see the gruesome work of the attackers when they drove past them. Unrecognizable as to sex or age, except for the stark whiteness under the bloody cast, there was no way to see them as being the remains of human beings.

"Oh, my God. They should be given a Christian burial," Mrs. Green gasped, holding a lace kerchief to her face.

"Ain't nothing we can do for them now," Wimbleton said and shook his head.

"Where's the Army?" Mrs. Green demanded.

"Off scratching their ass as usual," the other drummer said and then shook his head ruefully. "These devils are out for blood and we're all fools to even try to come up here. They're going to whip the Army's butt too."

Slocum didn't care whose butt they scratched or whipped; he wanted to be at the next station and his deepest concerns were over whether that place was still standing. He nodded to Judy, who looked shrunken beside him, a big girl turned small girl by the harsh twist of events in their lives. Where were the Sioux?

10

Rankin's station bristled with men armed with rifles. Many wore buckskin and looked to Slocum like a brigade. He soon learned they had a pack train of mules and were driven in there by a war party.

"Them angry Sioux sisters is all over them hills between here and there," a big man named Kelly said, holding his rifle by the muzzle with both hands.

"They killed an old boy riding on top," Slocum said, nodding toward the body wrapped in blankets on the ground near the coach.

"Who was he?"

"John Doe, I'd guess. He never spoke much and had the look of a man on the run."

Kelly kept trying to see something on the far ridge with a line of pines and cedar. "Them heathen bastards been building their nerve for weeks, I heard. They got a stage on up the way. It wasn't a pretty sight neither."

"I can imagine."

"They mutilated a white woman so bad my men got sick looking at her."

"They look pretty tough. You been trading with them?"

"Naw. I traded with the Crows and Shoshones. They hate them Sioux and they know what I do. So they'd like to slit my throat too."

Slocum nodded. "You seen anything yet?"

"Yeah, I see one of them." He stepped over, drew out a Sharps .50 caliber and set up a two-stick tripod. His shooting eye narrowed and a hush fell over the crowd when the first trigger clicked under his finger.

"Can't you see him mooning us with his bare ass?" Kelly asked.

Then the report of the .50 caliber deafened all of them standing around. In a cloud, the black gunsmoke drifted away and one of the buckskinners looking through a brass glass shouted, "Yeah, got him, Kelly."

"One less bare butt," Slocum said, familiar from his scouting days with the Army of the aborigine's practice of dropping their loinclothes at their enemies. This unfortunate one simply wasn't prepared for the range of Kelly's .50 caliber.

"Folks," Jim said, coming out of the low-walled stone-adobe structure. "I've got a schedule to keep."

"What are we going to do?" Judy asked Slocum.

"I guess go on to Deadwood."

She nodded and he helped her up into the coach.

The next stopover came before sundown and they changed drivers. Slocum was uncertain how anyone had managed to stay awake and drive as far as Jim and the Swede had. A black-haired man in a suit coat and wide-brimmed straw hat took over the driving chores. Layton's sombrero was secured by a leather chin-strap. His guard was a thin man in his thirties with a thick mustache. They called him Royal.

Royal quizzed Slocum about the Indian attack and nodded after he told him the story. "Shame that passenger got hisself shot."

"We're lucky that's all we lost."

"Reckon so. They don't do much at night, we should be in the hills by morning. Lots more soldiers up there too."

"Good."

"You know that guy, Kelly?" Royal asked under his breath.

"First time I've ever seen him."

"I got word he's been selling guns to them red devils for gold."

"He said he'd been trading with the Crows."

"Yeah, I would too. I think that shooting business a while ago here was just to take the suspicion from him."

"Load up!" Layton shouted from by the coach where he stood and Slocum herded Judy toward the stage.

"You believe him?" she asked under her breath.

"About Kelly?"

She nodded.

"It's hard to tell your enemies from your friends out here."

"Makes sense," she said.

Slocum looked back at the crew of buckskinners standing in a bunch in the sundown's red glow. Did Royal really know the truth about that bunch? No time to wonder, he had business to settle for her in Deadwood if they could get there.

The night passed swiftly, uneventful, and in the first daylight, shrouded by dark clouds, he leaned out from his side and could see the distant dark mounds they named the Black Hills, a place that the Sioux called their sacred place and where they said their gods resided. White men had replaced them in that temple with a new God they called gold.

"How much farther, Mr. Slocum?" Mrs. Green asked.

"Schedule says we'll arrive there late this afternoon."

"Oh, I must say, it has been a long ride."

"Yes, ma'am, a very long one. Is your husband waiting for you there?"

"No, my husband is dead. Mrs. Blaine and I are both widows and we are coming to build a church. A place of worship for all."

"I am certain that Deadwood can use one, ma'am."

"You would be welcome there, sir."

"Thanks for the invite."

"You too, young lady."

"Thanks," Judy said.

They changed stage horses at the next station and were back shortly on the road. Layton acted as if they were pressed to make it there close to the scheduled time. They passed a stagecoach headed southbound with a wave, and a hoot on the horn the guard used to notify the relay station ahead that they were coming, and to have the horses ready.

Most of the way-stops were run by tough former mountain men married to Indian women or breed squaws. Several boys usually worked about the place doing the physical jobs, like hitching the horses, while being directed by the man in charge. The matrimonial status of the women was no doubt a loose confederation. But the women covered the range from beautiful to fat, old and ugly, all of which had no application to the better than the bad food served by them.

The worst meal of the trip was a bowl of some strongly tainted stew with grease and animal hair floating on top. The best was some buffalo ribs, slow-cooked and flavorfully smoked, that a toothless stooped-back Indian woman served them on bark plates. They ate elk steaks, rice and corn bread for their last meal stopover at the base of the hills.

Slocum overheard the station-keeper ask Layton if they'd had any problems with Indians or robbers. The driver told the man about the passenger that had been killed and the troubles in the south.

"Be careful. They've been holding up the stages for what they can get off the passengers, they're so desperate."

"I will," Layton told the man and looked over at his guard. Royal nodded; he'd heard their conversation.

Back on their way, the road became twisted and the slopes soon were clad in thick ponderosa pines. One more change of horses and they would be there. Slocum was about asleep when the pop of a pistol drew him upright.

"Throw down your arms and raise your hands high."

"Don't do anything foolish," he said to the others. "They want your money and your jewelry. Not your life, if we act agreeable."

Both church women paled and the men nodded.

Someone jerked open the side door, stuck in a pistol muzzle and ordered them off. The robbers all wore flour-sack masks and canvas dusters to conceal their clothing. Two of them wore Hyer Kansas-made boots with square toes. The tallest one stood back, covered them and said nothing. There was something very familiar about him. Slocum wished he could see a distinguishing mark.

"All your jewelry and money," the short man said, holding open a sack for their deposits.

Judy put in a few dollars hesitantly and drew his glare from behind the mask.

"That's all you've got, lady?"

"All I've got in this world," she said indignantly.

"You, what've you got?" he asked Slocum.

"Twenty dollars, and two fifty-cent pieces."

"Yeah, I may search you."

"Go ahead."

The main man cleared his throat and, as if on signal, Shorty shrugged and went on, taking the widows' purses and then Wimbleton's meager offering.

"They're holding out on us," Shorty complained.

The head man made an impatient toss of his head and Slocum saw the engraved spurs on his boots when he turned to leave. He knew those hooks and who'd owned them last.

"All right, all right," Shorty mumbled, looking down in the sack. "But there ain't enough here to buy me one night's whiskey."

"You see something?" Judy asked as the robbers mounted up and prepared to ride off.

"Yeah," Slocum said quietly as thunder rolled across the hills. "That's Hash's gang."

"Oh."

The stage arrived in the deep canyon that housed Deadwood in a torrential afternoon downpour. Water ran down the sea of mud called a street, logs and planks made up the makeshift walks to carry foot commerce. A few hands waded about in the half-knee-deep muck, harnessing fresh horses for the turnaround.

They took their bags and Slocum pointed to a hotel across the street. "That looks good to me."

"Me too," she agreed.

The boards they chose looked stable enough to cross over upon and they started for the other side. The timbers were caked with lots of mud off the boots of other users. Somehow they made it over and were at last on the hotel porch out of the hard rain. But in the progress to reach that place they saw two others less fortunate fall off of other such structures into the mire and come up looking more like hogs than people.

Registered as man and wife, they ordered up a bathtub and lounged in their room, awaiting the tub's arrival as lightning flashed on the glass windowpane.

"Money still holding up?" he asked. "This is a rather expensive place to stay and I never asked before I signed us in."

"No problem, but I worried that robbers might search me for it."

Stretched out on his stiff back atop the bed, Slocum smiled. "All he needed was an excuse."

"You figure that's why Hash made him quit?"

"Maybe—Hash don't do much that don't work in his favor."

"How is that?"

"He may want to search you himself."

She blushed and shook her head, going to answer the knock on the door.

"Here's your tub," the youth announced and two maids with him carried in two pails of steaming water apiece.

"We'll be back with four more in a minute," the boy said and the women nodded at Slocum, setting down their loads.

"These men who have your brother again?" He sat on the bed and strained to pull off his first boot.

"Jake Hamilton and Farris Cunningham."

"You know what they do up here?"

"I suspect they run a gambling house."

"Your brother a gambler?"

"Not a good one."

Loud thunder overhead rattled the tin ceiling tiles and the flash lit up the whole room. More rain mixed with hail pelted the hotel's board-and-bat siding. The rest of their bathwater arrived and he gave them three empties to take back.

"I'll be back here in a half hour for the tub, etc. You can open the window and pitch the first water out. Just look that there ain't no one down there. Could get you shot."

Slocum agreed and closed the door after the boy and girl. When he turned back he saw Judy working frantically to get out of her travel-soiled dress. He smiled and began to undress himself.

"I don't know what's going to be best, the bath or a real meal."

"I know what will be fine," she said and winked wickedly at him, gingerly stepping into the tub. "That bed later on will be."

11

Slocum awoke early, dressed, slipped out of the room and left her to sleep while the sun tried to peek over Mount Mariah. Off-hours were the times to learn things. He needed some information about these guys Hamilton and Cunningham. On the boardwalk he found a small café and an empty stool. The waitress in her thirties took his order of eggs and ham.

"First time I seen you," she said and smiled.

"Won't be the last," he assured her and, after she nodded she had heard him, headed off with his order.

"New in town?" a grizzle-faced older man asked between spoons of oatmeal.

"Just got here. Where's the action?"

"Gambling? Up and down the gulch."

"Some high-rollers named Hamilton and Cunningham. You know them?"

The man squinched his right eye and looked hard at Slocum. "Pirates. You deal with them you better have knives and guns."

"I'd heard they were respectable businessmen."

"They damn sure ain't."

"Where could I find them?"

"White Elk Bar—half a block down on the right. But I'll warn ya, they're the crookedest deal in town."

"I appreciate the warning, but I promised a friend to look them up."

"Hmm, helluva friend, he must be." The old man went back to his cooked cereal.

The waitress returned with his eggs, ham and biscuits. She set down a mug of coffee and the platter in front of him and smiled. "Need more, the cook's got it back there."

"This will do."

"Pay on the way out." She left him a ticket.

A woman in her thirties, ample-bodied and attractive, she didn't miss flirting with the customers going down the counter.

"What's her story?" Slocum asked his companion.

"Neddy. Got two kids. Her old man ran off and left her."

"Nice lady."

The old man looked up and then he nodded. "Us guys make sure she don't suffer none. I figure the Sioux killed him. Anyone tries to cross the country around these damn hills except with an armed body of men is a damn fool."

"Yeah, they attacked the stage a day south of here."

"And where was the damn Army? Had their thumbs up their ass again." The old man shook his head in disgust.

Slocum nodded and busied himself with the food. He knew the woman's name—she might be a future source of information. Waitresses knew everything that went on in a town. He also knew the two behind Steven Steward's alleged problems were not well thought of by the populace. White Elk Bar came next.

He finished his meal, left her a tip, paid his bill and, picking his teeth with a toothpick, started downhill for the

White Elk Bar. Bleary-eyed swampers were busy emptying buckets of mop water in the street in front of the various establishments set up to deprive the miners of their pay and the prospectors of their free gold. Somehow this had become a custom of the frontier—be sure and fleece the workingman. They did that very thing in the cow towns where the cowboy arrived, dying of thirst and a hard-on too big to hide. They turned him out with a head-pounding hangover, his balls shriveled up in his scrotum, his pecker plugged with the clap and too broke to go back home to Texas. The mining-town dens of iniquity kept the laborers too broke to go home as well. After a night on the town, the prospector had to go back and rock his cradle some more to find the gold flecks for the next big party. As a brassy madam once said, that's what they expected, and they got a full dose of it.

A few brave souls were betting on the roulette wheel when Slocum entered the stale-smelling barroom and sauntered up to the bar. He ordered a beer from the crisp-mustached bartender then looked at himself in the mirror hanging over the back of the bar. Save for the four betters, the rest of the place was vacant.

"The second door on the right, head of the stairs. Maggie's always up by this time. She'll give you your money's worth in the sack, mister."

"Don't need any, but thanks. Hamilton or Cunningham around this hour?"

The barkeep frowned as if concerned that he would ask anything about them. "No. They expecting you?" he asked guardedly.

"I was told to look them up when I got here."

"You a gun hand?"

"Do I look like one?"

The man acted taken aback before he finally answered. "I ain't sure. No, you don't."

"Fine." Slocum'd seen enough and knew not to arouse any more suspicions. He paid the man and left the White Elk.

A half a block farther, he spotted the familiar roan horse standing hipshot with three other horses. Too good to be true, there was old roan—tied to the hitch rack. How far away was Hash?

He ducked inside the Stone Wall Saloon and let his eyes get accustomed to the dim lights. With his back to him, elbow on the bar, was that long drink of water, Hash.

"I'll take the roan back now," Slocum said, motioning to the barkeep to come down.

"Holy Cripes! What the hell are you doing here?"

"Come for my damn horse. Bring me a beer," he said to the short, swarthy-faced bartender. When the man was out of hearing, filling the mug, Slocum lowered his voice. "They've got Micheals in the Lodge Pole, Nebraska Jail."

"I heard that and it sure hurt me."

"Only way it would hurt is for you to lose that money you got in yesterday's stage robbery." Slocum moved in and rested his elbows on the bar.

"What're you talking about?"

"That was you ramrodding the deal."

"I never—"

"Lie to your wife, but don't lie to me. I seen them engraved spurs yesterday."

"I ain't got a wife."

Slocum saw by the look on Hash's face he'd knifed him deep about the spurs. But he had more important things to learn about. "I need to know about two guys, Cunningham and Hamilton."

"Tough bastards. They run the White Elk Bar and Casino. What you into them about?"

"They're holding a guy for ransom who owes them, I suspect a gambling debt."

"What's his name?" Hash asked, under his breath.

"Steven Steward. You know him?"

Hash looked around the noisy room to be certain they were alone. "Steward works for them. Didn't look like a captive to me."

"When did you see him last?"

"Yesterday, the day before." Hash raised the overflowing mug with suds spilling down the side.

"Must be a mistake."

"Maybe he was shaking down the family for more money."

Slocum set his glass down and wiped his mouth on the back of his hand. "You have a point."

"Damn, they caught Micheals. Dumb ass stayed in Kansas, didn't he?"

"I left him down by the Strip."

Hash looked in the mirror on the back of the bar and shook his head at himself. "I'll have to send him money for a lawyer."

"He'd appreciate that, I'm certain. Can you point out this Steward to me?"

"Sure, what the hell—all I've got to do is go buy me another damn horse."

"There is one more thing. There's an ex-Nebraska lawman named Piper who probably got him. He woke me up in that cathouse that next morning with a gun in my face—thinking I was you."

"Oh, shit, how did you get away?"

"Some precious dove turned us loose while they were busy sampling the free wares in the house."

"God bless them." Hash looked to the tin squares in the ceiling for heavenly intervention.

"Steward," Slocum reminded him.

"Let's wander down to the White Elk and see if he's there. Hey, these guys got real thugs on their payroll."

Slocum agreed, paid for their beers and started out after Hash. When they were out on the wooden boardwalk, Slocum checked around. "This business you're in doesn't look that healthy for no more than you're getting."

"Why, we got three watches, a ring and thirty dollars off your coach."

"Split four ways, that's hardly drover wages."

"It ain't going to make us rich. But the law up here is lax and who gives a damn? It'll have to do until I can do better."

"Your neck."

Hash ran his finger under the edge of his collarless shirt and looked uneasy at Slocum. "You make me feel nervous."

They pushed in the White Elk and immediately two girls came to meet them in short dresses with lots of their small cleavage showing. Hardly more than teens, they shared a brassy look and it was clear they had been at the game awhile.

"What'll it be gents?" the brunette said, catching the crook of Slocum's arm in hers.

"We just came by for a beer."

"Bring these gents a beer, Squirrely," she announced to the barkeep. "My name's Jenny and that's Hildy." She indicated the shorter sister on Hash's arm.

"Steward around?"

"Naw, he's gone to Lead on business. What you want him for?"

"Just talk," Hash said and looked over the smoky room at the rest of the crowd.

"Obviously you two don't need any services," Jenny said and smiled big.

"Not right now—but later . . ." Hash winked at them as they went away. He turned back to Slocum. "Well, is that good enough?"

Slocum studied his beer. This threw a whole new light on the subject—he wondered how Judy would take the news. Her brother wasn't any more a prisoner than nothing. A simple open-and-shut case of extortion. He hoisted the beer. "Good enough."

12

"You mean my brother works for them?" Judy looked shocked. She turned, shaking her head, and looked out their second-story window into the street below. "Father said he was no good, but to try and trick his own family . . ."

"We can get him up here and ask him."

"Yes, I'd like to face him and ask him why." She twisted around, nodding her head.

"It might not be nice."

"Damn, who cares about nice? Here I have been worried to death that we'd not get here in time to save him." Biting her upper lip, she charged across the room and threw her arms around Slocum. She buried her hard breasts into him and pressed her pelvis against his leg. "I'm so mad, I want to choke him to death."

"Won't do no good, and I even have my roan back. Found Hash and he led me to where your brother works as well."

"How and when can we confront him?" she asked, her thick lashes wet with tears.

"Find out where he lives and we'll jump him when he comes home."

"Good. I'll be ready to give him a piece of my mind. Is the roan all right?"

"Good as can be."

"I better plan to go back to Kansas after this is all over."

"Whatever you want to do."

"Right now—" She stepped back and undid his gun belt. Leaning against him, she brought it around to re-buckle it and then hang it on the straight chair back. "I think we need to play."

"Might not be half bad for us to do that." He swept her up and kissed her hard on the mouth. "In fact, I vote for it."

"Women can vote in Wyoming," she said, unbuttoning her blouse. "Can they here?"

"Sure, if they vote for this happening, I'd say give them two votes." He grinned big at her as the lovely pear-shaped breast spilled out for his exposure. "Maybe three."

They waited in the night shadows of the alley. A strong smell of garbage was in his nose. Some skinny cats pa-trolled the piles of waste, looking for a stray rat or mouse or any discarded food.

She tugged on his sleeve to indicate that the dark figure talking to himself was Steven. He sounded a little drunk and walked that way. When he went by them, she nodded to Slocum as they stood back in the darkness.

He used a key on the door lock and fought it until it fi-nally opened. Slocum was behind him and had his pistol out of his holster. "Make a single yelp and you're dead."

"Huh?"

"Just shut up and listen. One wrong move will be your last."

"I ain't got—"

"Shut up—" Slocum drove him inside and then she struck a match.

"Judy? What they hell are you doing here?" he gasped as she held up the candle lamp.

"I came to save my poor brother, you son of a bitch. Why did you do that? Send that letter saying you'd be killed if Father didn't pay them?"

He looked defeated. "He's got lots of money. I'm entitled to it. I'm his only son. What would it have hurt?"

"Hurt?" She pointed at her cleavage. Her eyes were hard slits glaring at him. "It didn't fool him. It hurt me and bad. I came up here to save you and learned you were nothing but a damn liar."

"That money is still mine."

She shook her head. "You won't ever get a cent of it."

"We'll see about that. Women ain't got no rights. It's the male heir gets the money."

"Maybe in Europe, but not in Kansas. He'll disown you as soon as I tell him what you did."

"Had enough?" Slocum asked her.

"Mind your own gawdamn business—"

Slocum jerked him up by a handful of his shirt and laid the gun barrel beside his cheek when he drew him up close to his face. "Listen and listen good. I ain't some dumb miner you can hardball. I'll slit your sack, stick your left leg through it and let you hobble back to the White Elk."

"Who—who are you?"

"My name's Slocum."

Steven nodded his head in submission. Slocum released him, slow like, at her words: "I've had enough of this coward."

"Coward!"

She whirled and pointed her finger. "Yes, you're a coward. You'd stayed home and worked you'd have inherited the whole thing. No, not you, you were afraid to do a little real work, to do anything except cheat folks out of their money. Change your name, you aren't good enough to wear the Steward name."

"Go to hell, you little bitch. You want his money, then keep it."

Slocum held the door open and when she went through it he emptied the cartridges from Steven's Colt onto the floor, then with a kick sent the gun skittering across the room. "Try anything and you're dead."

He closed the door. They hurried down the alleyway.

"What now?" he asked her.

"I'll catch the next stage back to Cheyenne."

"Want me to go along?"

"Yes, but you don't have to. I'm a big girl." They moved into the light coming out on the porches from the saloons and weaved through the foot traffic headed for the hotel.

"I can take you back to Cheyenne."

"No, you have enough problems. Besides, that lawman Piper who's looking for you might be down there by now. I'll take the stage back by myself tomorrow. Tonight we can play games."

"Yes," he agreed, exchanging a smile with her.

In the morning he put her on the Cheyenne-bound stage. She paid him two hundred dollars for his trouble, despite his pleas that it was too much. He watched the rocking coach head out and drew a deep breath of the pine-scented air. One thing for certain, he'd miss her.

An hour later he was playing dime-ante poker in the Red Horse with some freighters. Cards were smiling on him and by mid-afternoon he had a small pile of winnings. Talk was about the angry Sioux, Cheyenne and Araphos and what they'd do next.

"Seen two wagon trains coming up here they wiped out. Wasn't pretty," Bill Guffy said, a man in his fifties. "Freighting ain't worth losing your life over. Hell, there's civilized places to work. I don't need no damn arrows in my back."

"Army ain't doing a thing," Wooster grumbled across the table. "What do you think, Slocum?"

"It sure ain't over with them, despite the government saying they bought it."

"Over? Bought it, my ass," McCoy grunted. "Hell, boys it's just begun and going to get lots worse. Mark my words. Why, taking over these hills is like a festering boil to the renegades, and its ready to pop."

"Three sevens," Slocum said, showing his hand.

"Damn, you're lucky this evening." Wooster shook his head. The long locks of snowy, curly hair danced on his shoulders.

"Put his woman on the coach for Cheyenne and got serious about card playing is all," Guffy said.

"Purty as she was, I'd be crying in my beer," McCoy added and discarded his hand in disgust.

"What're you doing next?" Guffy asked.

"Looking for more work."

"Two things you can do up here. Either pan for gold or rob them that does."

Everyone laughed. Wooster finished shuffling the cards and began dealing out the next hand after they all pitched in their ten-cent ante.

"You seen Wild Bill lately?"

Slocum shook his head. "I knew him in Abilene."

"He's a shadow of the man he was then," Wooster said, setting the deck down to look at his hand. "He's drinking hard and savage to anyone gets in his way. Far cry from the lawman in Abilene. Some say its over his wife—you know she's a circus performer."

Slocum shook his head; he'd not heard about the ex-lawman's marriage.

"Good-looking gal. Seen her picture in tights."

"Bill's probably up there in Number Nine Saloon playing cards right now."

Slocum nodded to Wooster and drew two new cards. By Guffy's raise, he figured he'd better be hitched with a real hand. Nothing came in the draw, so when Guffy raised again he folded and pitched his hand in.

"I better get some business done today," Slocum said, standing up and pocketing his winnings.

"What's that?" McCoy teased.

"Oh, check on my roan horse, for one."

"Come back and play with us."

"I'll do that."

The others wished him well and he left the saloon. At the livery he found the roan chomping on hay and, satisfied, went on up the hill. On the boardwalk and porches, he strode past the Number Nine. He and Wild Bill never were thick friends so he kept going. Another thing niggling him if he stayed much longer, he'd soon need to find a room in a boardinghouse. The hotel was too expensive to live in.

He slept another night in the bed that still smelled of Judy's musk. In his tossing and turning he dreamed of having her creamy skin under his palm, the tight muscles of her stomach, her silky powerful legs and the pulsating walls of her vagina. He awoke at dawn with a painfully stiff hard-on and grinned down at it—damn, he really would miss her.

After a sponge bath at the pitcher and basin, he dressed and went to breakfast at the café down the hill. The same waitress brought his order and whispered her street address when she bent over to put the plate before him. He nodded that he'd heard her. She also gave him a peek at her deep cleavage—then she was gone.

After his meal, he decided to take the roan out and see

the country. He rode in a wide circuit and saw plenty of men panning the creeks. Hard-looking, unshaven men standing in water to their knees and hoisting up shovels full of gravel into a sluice. Some wore gum hip boots, others rolled up their pant legs and went into the streams barefoot.

No great urge to get off and join them consumed Slocum. A few would find some big nuggets but they'd spend it all on pussy and booze and shortly be broke like they wanted to be and chase down more. There was every language spoken there was as well as some celestial who's ques swung with their stiff work ethics. Talking like magpies in some Chinese dialect, they worked like ants on the dredges others heaped up.

Slocum was back in Deadwood outside the stable when a rider came charging on a lathered horse into town.

"The stage! Them red devils got the stage yesterday."

"What're you talking about?" he demanded.

"The stage left yesterday. It's burned up and left to rot down south." The youth bailed off his out-of-wind horse and spoke to the livery man. "Get me a fresh one, I've got to tell the Army."

"Were there any bodies?" Slocum insisted.

"Yeah, the driver guard and two passengers."

"You see the body of a woman there?" Slocum had him by the arm for an answer as the crowd began to gather.

"You mean the Kansas woman?"

"How did you know that?"

"Fred at the Acuff station asked me the same thing. Must have been a looker. No, no sign of her there."

Slocum backed off. They must have taken her captive. Damn. He'd need a pack outfit and a tracker—he wished he'd gone along at least part of the way. Now the renegades had her.

He pushed himself through the angry mob gathering in

the street. They'd do nothing but talk and cuss. He would need supplies—always some hope that they took her as a slave when they finished gang-raping her. Judy was no slacker; she wouldn't die easy.

"You heard the news?" Hash asked as Slocum went by him.

"They've got Judy."

"The woman—aw, hell, what a shame. Where the hell are you going?"

"To get her back."

"Alone?"

"You're looking at my posse."

"You're crazy."

"Maybe, but I'm also serious."

"Wait, I'll go along. I owe you."

Slocum shook his head. "What about your gang?"

"Hell, that's getting boring. I missed the gold shipments three times this week alone."

"Someone else get them."

"Yeah, the Green Gang."

Slocum laughed. "You guys lined up in a row to rob the damn stages?"

Hash made a disgusted scowl and fell in beside him. "I guess."

"You know what the chances are for getting her back alive?"

"Little to none?"

Slocum nodded and tossed his head toward Ralston's Mercantile. "You got a rifle?"

"Yeah." Hash followed him over the precarious boards spanning the muddy street.

"Good," he said. The bell rang over his head as they entered the store.

In ten minutes, he had a pannier full of flour, rice, baking powder, bacon, dried apples, raisins, jerky, lard, coffee, air-tight tomatoes and peaches, along with some brown sugar. He found a dutch oven and coffeepot, two tin plates and cups and utensils, two boxes of .44/40 cartridges for the used rifle he picked out and two more packs of .45 ammo for the Colt.

The livery man sold them a brown mustang mare for twenty bucks and while Hash rode after his things, Slocum led the mare off the roan back to the store. With her under the pack saddle, he started south to find Hash. The posse of fifty or so riders had already left town in a flurry of mud-splashing hooves. All flash and dash, in twelve hours they'd be worn out and still no Indians in their sight.

Hash joined him in the south part of town. He rode a long-headed racehorse, a deep brown bay, and the animal looked built for speed. A bedroll on behind flopped up and down in the tie-down strings while the stock of Hash's rifle stuck out of the scabbard.

"I won't miss this place," Hash said in disgust.

"You may on the trail of these redskins."

"I'll tell you when I do."

"What did you tell the gang?" Slocum checked around to be certain they had not drawn any tagalong or anything out of order.

"Told them I was leaving—to kiss my ass."

"They do it?" Slocum chuckled.

"Hell, no, they said good, they were tired of splitting the pot with me anyway."

"One way to leave friends. We better trot the horses or we'll never get there."

Late afternoon they found the last stopover that the stage had made before the raid. The man in charge told them all he knew. A few miles south the Indians had struck, used the morning sun in the stage occupants' eyes, and slaughtered them, burning the coach and taking the woman, for there was no sign of her body.

"They probably raped and killed her by now, on the run and all."

"Something we aim to find out," Slocum said and they rode on.

They found the posse camped at the massacre site and, as Slocum thought, both men and horses were worn out, no supplies and ready to return to Deadwood.

"I don't guess there's a helluva lot we can do for her," the lawman said. "If she is alive. Few women live more than twenty-four hours on the war-path trail. Guess we'll let the Army settle it with them."

Slocum nodded that he heard him, sitting his horse as the blood-red light of sundown touched the peaks to the west. Then he booted the roan on with a head toss to Hash.

"Everyone acts like we ain't going to do any damn good," Hash said, spurring his horse up with the roan.

"Everyone ain't cut out to find her either."

Hash twisted in the saddle and looked back at the worn-out, dismounted posse. "They sure ain't."

The tracks were obvious and they led west into the hills. Slocum knew from the scattered horse-droppings on the trail that the war party was on the move, and it meant they weren't taking much time to stop. They might not take a break for forty miles, then, if they saw no dust of pursuit, they'd take on a more leisurely movement. Also, there were companies of soldiers patrolling the vast region along the Dakota-Wyoming borders, which could spook them. The thing that niggled him the most was the fact that, in times of an attack on them, they usually killed their white hostages.

"They headed for the Powder River?" Hash asked.

"I would judge that's where the rest of the tribe is out looking for buffalo."

"What did they get off that stage—I mean besides her?"

"A few weapons, some mail to start fires and the satisfaction they disrupted something of the white man's, I guess."

"A freight train I could see, but a stage—don't make sense."

"Lot's of things don't make sense. They're angry and mad and want revenge on whatever they can attack with the least losses."

"It's about pitch dark. We going to stop somewhere tonight?"

"How about on the next flat we reach?"

"Fine with me."

Dawn came on a cool breath. Both men rubbed the grit out of their eyes and rolled up their bedcovers. On his feet, Slocum tried to straighten the stiffness out of his back with his hands on his hips. The effort didn't help. They gnawed on jerky, saddled the horses and rode on.

Mid-morning, they found a pool of water. Their horses gratefully slurped up their share and Slocum refilled their canteens. A vast sagebrush sea stretched westward before them toward the Powder. The land rolled in gray-purple waves sliced by deep cuts of dry washes. Pony tracks went that way too.

They had a jerky breakfast and also a can each of tomatoes slurped down on the run. Before he mounted Slocum broke open a few horse biscuits from the ground after saddling the horses. The fact that they were still damp inside meant Slocum and Hash were less than twenty-four hours behind them.

"We may catch up with them," Slocum said, stepping in the saddle.

"What then?"

He shook his head. "I guess do whatever we have to do."

"Twenty or thirty bucks?"

"More like a dozen."

"Yeah, but that's six to one."

"You want out?"

"Hell, no."

"Let's ride then."

They trotted off with the sun on their backs.

"One thing, Slocum. We don't catch up with them today, we stop and cook some food and make us some coffee. My teeth are about to float out of my mouth for some."

Mid-afternoon, Slocum reined up and frowned. "You smell some smoke?"

Floured in the fine dust, Hash narrowed his lashes and reined up his horse. He shook his head, testing the air.

"Where would they be?"

"In one of the deep washes. They sure ain't up on top." Slocum stood in the stirrups and sniffed the air—nothing but the tang of sage.

A horse whined in the distance and Slocum was off on his feet, holding both animals from making a sound.

"I heard that too." Hash muzzled his gelding and looked around like a man searching for the source when he heard a rattler buzz.

"Lets hobble these ponies in the wash behind us and go on foot."

"Gawd almighty, we about rode up on them?"

"We may have."

Hash looked back over his shoulder, then he fell in behind Slocum as he led his two animals off the steep bank.

"Wonder how many there are left?"

"No telling."

"Jeez, the damn hair on my neck's standing straight up."

"We must be close then." Slocum stuck his boot heels in the loose dirt to keep his balance going downhill. The horses slid down with him.

Their animals hobbled and out of sight, they extracted their rifles from their scabbards. Slocum tossed Hash a box of cartridges. "Don't waste 'em."

Hash nodded with his mouth set in a tight line. Slocum went past him and started back up the steep cow's-face side of the draw. *Judy, we're coming.*

13

Belly down between the gnarled sagebrush, Slocum could see their hipshot ponies on the dry gulch floor. In the shade of the high cut side, several blankets were spread and bucks lounged about on them. Where was she at?

There was a small fire, the one he no doubt had smelled, and something in a kettle cooking over it. A buck squatted by the pot as if tending to the food preparation. There were guns in the camp and some lances lying near their owners. But no sign of Judy.

If they had any goods to show for their raid, they must be the two big horses, obviously a stage-line team in the midst of the pony herd. The mustangs looked gaunt and done in—perhaps the reason why the war party rested, feeling secure there was no pursuit.

"Where is she?" Hash hissed.

"Someone must have taken her off."

Hash nodded. "When we start shooting, we take as many as we can and finish on the horses?"

"We better make them count."

Slocum reached back, drew out his Colt and set it beside

him on the ground. He rolled over on his back and checked the chamber.

"Go."

He took the left side. His first shot took a large buck and dropped him. Number two took out one going for his rifle. Confusion set in on the party of bucks under the heavy barrage of lead. Hash's shots were counting, and the rest of them left their weapons and ran for their horses.

The ones they mounted were either shot out from under them or the riders were shot off of their backs. In a matter of minutes, the handful left standing gave up and raised their hands. In wide-eyed shock, they cried out for surrender and the two rifles went silent—save for the hurried reloading clicks of the two men.

"Get down here where we can see you," Slocum shouted, motioning with his gun barrel for them to come away from the horses.

Staggering in the sand they came back as directed.

"Sit on the ground," Slocum ordered, watching them drop to their butts obediently.

"You going down?" Hash asked.

"Yeah, keep them covered."

"Reckon they know where she is?"

"They may not tell us."

"Yeah, if'n they ain't already cut her throat."

Slocum found a tough place to come off the wall. He half-slid part of the way down on his butt and about went face-first once, but managed to recover his balance for the last part of the descent. On the wash floor, he cautiously looked around. Then he kicked the weapons away from the dead and wounded as he circled the five left.

"Where is she at?" he demanded.

No answer.

"Where is the white woman?"

Downcast, they made no reply.

"Who wishes to die next?"

"The white woman is gone with Bull Elk," one of the loincloth-wearing teenagers said; obviously he knew English.

"He the chief?"

"Sleeping Bear is chief, Bull Elk a medicine man." The boy shrugged.

"Where did he go?"

"Powder River." The youth looked hard at the ground between his brown knees.

"How far ahead is he?"

The youth shook his braids as the out-of-breath Hash came off the bank and joined Slocum.

"What do they know?"

"A medicine man, Bull Elk, has taken her to the Powder River."

"How do you know that ain't some lie?"

"Don't. Gather up their weapons. We'll have to shoot the horses if we don't take them with us."

"We ain't leaving them anything?"

"A few bows and arrows to kill game is all."

"Holy shit, this is a brand-new rifle." Hash held up the lever action long gun he'd picked up from the ground and shook his head. "Better damn gun than I've got."

"Where's the gold?" Slocum demanded from the boys.

Hash stopped and frowned at the question. The young Indians looked hard at each other. At last the speaker said, "Over by the horses."

In an instant, Hash tore out for the herd, churning sand with his boot soles. Slocum kept his rifle leveled at the prisoners. Hash dropped on his knees and opened the broken-latched strongbox.

"We're rich, Slocum!" He held up white canvas pouches of obvious gold. "Gawdamn. We're rich as hell!"

Slocum nodded that he'd heard his partner and turned back to the boys. "What were you going to do with it?"

"Buy more guns."

"Where and when."

"Traders bring guns in a few days for gold."

"What are their names?"

"Cunting-ham."

Flush with the excitement of their find, Hash staggered back over with the heavy chest to show him the loot.

"You hear him?" Slocum scowled at the bucks.

"No." Hash blinked at him.

"Cunningham is the one that trades them the guns for the gold."

Hash narrowed his eyes and he shook his head. "That bastard."

"Get our horses and some to pack that out on," Slocum said, holding the rifle on the prisoners.

Their own horses brought over, the gold and firearms were packed on two of the stage-line horses. Then Hash took a youth with him and they caught the Sioux horses. They hitched the rest of them leads to tails to take the herd with them. For security purposes, the prisoners' hands were tied behind their backs; the restraints would keep them there long enough for them to get gone. Slocum climbed into the saddle and they hurried out of camp, Hash looking over things and bringing up the rear. He whipped the ponies with a quirt to hurry the train along.

"Where're we headed?" he shouted when the last pony clamored up on the top of the bank.

"We have ten days, the boy said back there, before Cunningham brings the rifles to trade."

"Dark of the moon, huh?"

"Yeah, so the Army don't get wise to them."

"What're we going to do about them?"

"I'd like to give them a real reception if we can find her and get back in time."

Hash looked back over his shoulder then straightened in the saddle. "How long we keeping these dumb ponies?"

"A ways farther, then we can turn them loose."

"Good." He turned out and rode to the back to quirt the laggers some more.

By evening, after scattering the ponies, they set up camp at a water hole, cooked some bread, fried some bacon and made coffee.

"We must have forty thousand in gold."

Slocum looked across the smoky fire and nodded. "More money than I could ever use."

"Yeah, it would bring down the law faster than a shot, wouldn't it?"

"It would do that." Slocum wiped his bristled mouth on his calloused palm. "Damn shame, ain't it?"

"Yeah, we got less than three hundred out of that Lodge Pole Bank in Nebraska. Here we are with more gold than we could spend and can't even consider it, can we?"

"Them lawmen wait outside them fancy cathouses in Denver for the next fool to come along and throw a big party with his proceeds. 'Course they let them spend a big part of it first."

"Whew, a man could stuff his old tool in some dandy pussies with this kind of money."

"You could think about them the whole time you were in one of them territorial prisons too."

"Jacking off." Hash broke into laughter. "What do we do with it?"

"We may need it to buy her back."

In the falling twilight, Hash looked pained at him. "How do we do that?"

"I ain't sure yet. But this Sleeping Bear needs that gold to get his guns. I'd say we can swap it for her."

"And not get killed?"

"That's what I'm working on."

"Work hard on it. I like living too well to give up on it now. Especially with this much gold on hand."

"I'll do that." Slocum took another swig of the coffee. It tasted good. *Judy, you keep believing we're coming for you.*

14

"Oh, damn!" Hash swore at the sight of the column of cavalry appearing out of the north. Staffs flapping, they came by two's in a short lope.

"No need to do anything but meet them," Slocum said in surrender.

"What about the gold?"

"Don't tell them. It's hid well enough in our pannier."

"Hell, they're bound to be curious."

"Then don't act concerned about it. Otherwise you'll tip them off we have something to hide."

"Ho!" the officer called out. His gauntlet held up, he stopped his company.

The lieutenant, a scout in buckskins and a sergeant rode over. They nodded and drew up. Slocum recognized the scout as Harry Keller.

"Morning," the officer offered.

"Morning," Slocum said. "We're looking for a medicine man called Bull Elk. You haven't seen him?"

The lieutenant turned to the noncom and the man shook his head.

"We don't know him. Why are you looking for him?" the officer asked.

"Him and his band robbed a Deadwood-Cheyenne stage and took a white woman off it. We recovered the two horses and some guns from stragglers in his bunch." Slocum tossed his head toward the two big horses. "But we haven't caught him yet."

"Keller, you know these men?" the West Pointer asked.

"I do Slocum here. He was a good scout with Custer in Kansas."

The officer nodded as if taking that under consideration. "What about their story, Sergeant Mhoon?"

"They've been on the run and they didn't get those shields and brass-tacked rifles off no settlers," the noncom said, standing in his stirrups to better see their things.

"Hey, there's a white woman in the hands of these hostiles and we're burning daylight sitting here," Slocum said.

"I seriously doubt she's survived."

"Listen mister, your opinion is yours. I want her back. You can either take up this Bull Elk's tracks or go your merry way. What will it be?"

"Keller, you see any signs?" The scout had made a good circle down the trail and was returning.

"Yeah, sir, there's tracks going west of five unshod ponies."

"We will join you then, sir."

"Good. Slocum's my name. Charlie Hash's my partner." He gave a thumb toss at the stone-faced Hash, who was holding his reins and the saddle horn in both hands.

"Deering's mine, Sergeant Mhoon and you know Keller."

Slocum agreed and the officer sent the noncom after the company. They loped off to the west. Slocum noticed Hash's shoulders drop an inch with the pressure off of them and the man relaxed into the rocking gait. No one else must have noticed. Both men shared a private nod and they hurried off at the head of the column of troopers.

"Nice to have this many guns with us," Hash finally said.

"Real nice."

Alternating between loping, trotting and walking, by the time the red ball began to fall behind the horizon, they'd made close to forty miles, by Slocum's consideration. The Powder River had to be close when they stopped for the night.

Keller ambled over and squatted down by Slocum's and Hash's fire. "We're ten or some miles from the river. Moon gets up, I'm going scouting for their camp. Want to go along?"

Slocum nodded and poured the scout more coffee in his cup. "I'd like her alive."

"I savvy alive, but you know—"

"I know, but I've rode a lot of miles to not give up on the idea now."

"In twenty minutes, let's ride?"

Slocum agreed and the scout moved off with a thanks for the coffee.

"We must have better coffee than them soldiers got." Hash smiled in the firelight. "I sure never figured that plan of yours would work this slick."

Slocum nodded that he'd heard him, then he reached for the pot and poured himself another cup. For certain, ahead of him would be a lengthy night out there with Keller. How long since he'd scouted for Custer in Kansas? Ten years earlier, he still recalled the arctic-like conditions and how they'd plowed through the knee-deep white stuff looking for the Cheyenne on the Quachita.

Custer had held no respect for trooper or horse. He was

a man over-possessed with finding their winter camp and a fight, too long put off by the inclement winter weather and the vastness of the territory. He'd outrun his supply wagons, floundering in the drifts far at his rear, in his obsessive flight to strike upon the hostiles, who were still out there beyond his grasp. Then, when they did find them, the Cheyenne had outnumbered them three to one. Despite his own scouts' dire warnings of this larger force, he'd gone ahead with a manic plan to attack them. To open the fight, Custer had ordered them to fire on the American flag waving over the old chief's lodge.

"Shoot that lying red bastard—he probably killed ten white men to get it!" Custer'd sworn, when a noncom had complained about the obvious.

Under the howitzers' blasts, the brevetted general had even scoffed at the scouts' reports of the many hostiles in the valley. But when the fighting had broken out, the number of Cheyenne braves ready to fight while their women and children fled had quickly proven to be greatly underestimated. Things had gone from bad to worse for the Seventh, until at last, in the face of an impending disaster, Custer had pulled everyone back from the overwhelming forces that were decimating his ranks. Moving to the north, Slocum had heard the bitter talk whispered among the enlisted men over leaving their dead on the field for the squaws to mutilate.

"The damn supplies never got there!" Custer had shouted to silence his opposition. "If we'd had enough ammo, we'd have blasted their red asses to kingdom come."

George Armstrong could bald-facedly lie to experienced fighters like the men of the Seventh Cav, but he couldn't expect them to believe a word of the angry oration in his own defence. "Ole Glory Boy" had had his way and needlessly wasted many a good man on the bloody battle-

field that frozen day. The hard-eyed troops had ducked
their heads against the sharp wind and their tails between
their horses' legs as they'd retreated to Fort Supply—
choking on the disgust and bitterness swelling their hearts.
"Play the 'Garry Owen' for the brave dead and God bless,"
them had been the words on their chapped lips.

Now Slocum stared into the night and listened to a
prairie wolf howl off in the darkness. He rose to his feet. At
least it wasn't freezing out there in the Wyoming
Territory—how many Sioux were ahead in their camp on
the Powder River? In a couple of hours he'd know. *Damn
Judy, I'm coming.*

15

"See anything of her?" Keller whispered as the two men bellied down on the low rim that ran along the east side of the Powder River bottoms. The camp size looked larger then Slocum had expected. There were plenty of Sioux in the camp, men, women and children. Several fires blazed up, giving some light and illumination. He knew that to see her amongst that many would be hard. They no doubt had her dressed in Indian rags by this time, which would make identifying her even harder.

"Nothing. But I didn't expect to."

"I ain't sure that shave-tail from West Point wants to tangle with this many red niggers at one time." Keller shook his bearded face. "They might eat him and spit the rest out." The scout chuckled as if amused at the notion.

"What if we take the horse herd and run them off? That would leave them a foot, save for a few ponies in camp."

"Hell, you're talking about work."

"We had their horses, we could dicker with them for her."

"I like my ass and hair too well to try something like that."

Slocum looked over at the scout with a scowl. "Well you can ride back to camp then. I'll be along driving those ponies after you."

"You're crazy."

"I may be crazy, but it's the only way I stand a chance to get her out of there alive."

"Jeez, oh, Jessie. You're serious about this horse-stealing, ain't yeah?" Keller closed his eyes and shook his head in disbelief.

"They ain't got anything but young boys guarding that pony herd."

"Why, they'll be mad as hornets."

Slocum looked, pained, at the man. "Who gives a shit?"

"How're you going to do it?" Keller asked, moving with him as they eased back from the rim.

"Scout out the nighthawks and take them out. Then we stampede the whole herd east toward your outfit."

"We get caught, it'll be our asses."

"I don't aim to get caught." Slocum unhitched the roan and bounded into the saddle. Keller could gripe or come on—he didn't have time for his pussyfooting around.

"I'm coming—"

They found the four boys herding the large herd. Slocum snuck up and grabbed the first one from behind, clamping his hand over the youth's mouth. In minutes they had him gagged and bound. The next one came by riding his horse and nodding his head, half asleep. He awoke wide-eyed, looking at the two white man pinning him on the ground and stuffing a rag into his mouth before he could yell. Having him well tied up, and moving low, they skirted the hoof-shuffling herd and found number three sound asleep. With him bound and gagged too, only one was left.

Keller caught the boy's reins and Slocum jerked him off the horse. The boy yelped, but with no one else that mattered close enough to hear him, they soon had him silenced and hobbled him tight.

Slocum sent Keller for their own horses while he watched the distant lights of the campfires. Sleeping Bear would have something to think hard about come daylight. There must be over two hundred head in the herd that the starlight danced on.

"Here." Keller delivered the reins and both men mounted, listening to the *mmm's* of the boys straining at their binds.

"You'd think they wanted loose," Keller said under his breath and the two spread out.

Pistol in his hand, Slocum looked at his partner. Keller nodded and the report of their six-guns awoke the ponies. Heads flew up and the loud *eeha's* sent them driving toward the dark horizon where the sun would emerge in a few hours.

The Sioux's transportation left, driven by their shrill screams and wild abandonment. They tore out, pushed by both men at their rear and more gunshots to punctuate the night. Flowing like a great blanket, they ran free across the rolling prairie guided by the two riders, in a direction that was generally eastward, as well as could be gauged in the pearly light. Over a thousand hard-driving hooves stirred up the fragile ground so that the fleeing band left a great cloud of dust in their wake that made the driving job even more difficult for the two men.

Waving his arm and shouting at his wards, a smile crossed Slocum's slick lips. This might be the greatest horse theft ever perpetrated against the Sioux in their lifetime. In the past they would never have left four boys to guard them. But who would steal them? The Cheyenne were their allies, the Arapahos, no problem and the Crow too cowardly to come this far into enemy land. The days of horse thieves were over—or so Sleeping Bear must have thought when he went to sleep that night.

The horses kept running as if the excuse to do so only encouraged them more. Slocum sought a high spot out of the dust, to look for any pursuit. But in the black-and-white night he saw no movement on their heels.

They pushed on until the peach light began to crease the horizon.

"Camp's that way." Keller pointed to the south when Slocum reined up before him.

"They're about run out. I think they'll stay in a bunch. Go tell the lieutenant we've got his Christmas present up here."

Keller shook his head like he didn't believe it. "I never figured we'd get this done and live to talk about it."

"It ain't over yet," Slocum cautioned him and stood in the stirrups to check their back trail. "Ride."

Keller left, spurring his lathered pony for camp. Slocum let the hard-breathing roan walk around the perimeter of the herd. Stallions fought and kicked one another. One tried to breed a mare, but was knocked off by another. The second stud needed little teasing to run his long dong out and climb onto his prize. Hunching his great dick past her furious tail into her pulsating cunt, he soon was jumping forward on his hind legs, biting her on the neck so she squealed in protest. At last he gave a deep grunt and came inside her, slowly going limp and coming off, his appendage leaking cum out of the sunflower-sized head.

The mare squatted and pissed a great spray of yellow

urine. Stud number two was not to be denied and came on his hind feet to copulate with her. In an instant he was humping it to her, and came too. Before the irritated mare could recover from her second screwing, a third stud, an aggressive black piebald, mounted her. She staggered under his force and tried to dance out from underneath him, but he screamed with vengeance, pounding his huge black-and-white dick into her. She went to her knees, but he reached down with his flashing teeth, caught her by the mane and neck then he drew her back up to finish his business with a great drive that left him played out.

Head hung to the ground, the tired mare threatened to fall down on her wobbly legs. No more studs tried her again. But her sisters in the herd were being raped at the same time by others. The males no doubt had been awakened sexually by the hard drive and the females coming into heat caused a great breeding affair—that, plus fighting by the studs, their screams being carried in the cool air.

Slocum was grateful when the officer and a handful of men rode out with Keller.

Lieutenant Deering stood up in the stirrups, used a gauntlet to shade his eyes to look over the herd and then shook his head in disbelief. "How did you do this?"

"Caught up the nighthawks, tied them up and drove them here."

"I've been looking for these hostiles for weeks. Never even got close and you go in one night and steal all their damn horses. You need work?"

"No, I need a white captive and I'd bargain for her with them if you'd let me. Might save her life."

"You have twelve hours. Then I shoot the horses. Those are my orders."

"What if they'll go back with you?"

Deering looked perplexed for a moment then he recovered and spoke. "Then I'll spare only the ones they need to ride in on. What do you plan to do?"

"I plan to go in under a white flag and palaver with them."

"Why, they'll kill you."

"They ain't holding the high card. Let me do what I have to do to get her out—if'n she's still alive, and any others that are in there too. Then we can discuss what to do next."

The young officer looked satisfied when he nodded sharply. "But you tell them if they kill you or any of the hostages I'll kill every damn horse here."

"I understand." He booted the roan into the herd and lassoed a high-headed, obviously hot-blooded horse. "You keep the roan for when I come back." He handed the lead to the noncom.

"You're either a damn fool or the bravest man I ever met," the Irish sergeant said in his brogue, as Slocum switched his saddle to the new horse.

"I ain't the bravest, Sarge, for damn sure." He made two tries, then swung his leg over and sat in the seat.

"By me, yeah are. Be careful lad and get her back. I'd hate meself to have to shoot all these ponies tonight."

Slocum waved to them and set the pacing horse out for the Powder River. The big bay ate up ground just as he expected him to. He knew he'd meet the bucks that were trailing the herd somewhere ahead. With the warm sun on his back, he thought about stopping and sleeping for a few hours—time that he did not have to squander.

Down the grades and up the other side, the gelding's long legs reached out in great ground-gaining strides that he did so effortlessly. No doubt stolen from a white man, the bay was eating up miles. Slocum kept his gritty eyes pealed for any sign, any movement that represented the trackers, and urged him on.

Then, like magic, they appeared on the rise ahead. First one, then more hatless figures on multicolored ponies pulled up.

Slocum reined the big horse to a halt in the dry wash, jerked the rifle out of the scabbard and felt for the white cloth in the saddlebags. Not looking away from them, he drew it out and tied it onto the gun's muzzle. He shifted both hands, checked the chamber to be certain he had a bullet in there then drove the lever back, satisfied it was loaded. The rifle butt balanced on his knee, his white flag barely fluttering. He advanced on the dozen or so bucks stopped on the rise. Even in the distance he could read the confusion on their faces—it was sink or swim for him.

16

"Who in the gawdamn hell are you?" the black-faced buck on the yellow paint demanded.

Good, they spoke English, or one did anyway.

Slocum balanced the Winchester's butt on his knee and reined up the bay. "Slocum. I came to trade several hundred horses for the white captives in your camp."

The hard-eyed translator told the others sitting their mounts his words. They laughed and then, one-handed, pointed their rifles at him and made sounds from their mouth like they had shot him.

"Tell them that all their horses will be shot if I am harmed."

With a smug look of "I'll humor you for this," the translator spoke to the others.

They belly-laughed at him and several more made vocal shots at him.

"You are stupid, white man. We know there is only one more of you. We can read tracks. How many horses can he kill before we swoop down on him?"

Slocum nodded. "Those trackers are from Keller."

"Killer, you say." The translator told them and they laughed more."

"You know who he is?"

"Yeah, big horse killer."

"No, he's an Army scout. The Army has your horses."

"Huh?" His face drawn up in a rage, the translator drove his paint in close and put the muzzle of his rifle in Slocum's face.

"If I die, then you have no horses," Slocum said, smelling the spent gunpowder from the bore and the rancid bear grease on the man's body.

The translator fought the horse back and looked hard at Slocum as if in deep consideration. He didn't speak for a long moment—then with a toss of his head for them to pull back, he broke into Sioux. They were harsh words he spoke and the others had to rein up their ponies as they listened intently.

More was spoken in private by the various members as if they feared he knew their dialect. Dark hate filled their eyes, which kept darting looks at him, while the situation was discussed between the dozen or so obvious leaders of the band who had kept a horse in camp.

At last, the translator nodded in agreement with them; then he booted his horse toward Slocum. He stopped a few feet short.

"We have no white captives."

"I want the woman that Bull Elk took from the Deadwood stage."

He pursed his thick copper lips and shook his head. "There is no one."

Slocum nodded that he had heard him. His guts roiled. His next move might get him shot down or it would show them he meant business. One or the other. His palms felt wet, but he had no plans to show them anything, least of all

to dry them. He lifted the reins, used his heel to make the
bay turn around to leave.

"Then you have nothing to trade for them and the horses
will be shot."

"Wait—"

He halted the horse. The skin on his neck crawled. With
his back to them, he didn't know if they'd shoot him or
want to negotiate more. The gauntlet was down.

"Wait. We need to talk more."

Gently he turned the bay back. He noticed that they
were in a tight huddle on the ground, holding their jawbone
bridle reins to their mounts and everyone talking at once.
Somewhere off in the sagebrush a magpie called and then
another answered.

At last, with much head-shaking, they sat down cross-
legged, save for one of the younger ones who jumped on
his pony and raced back toward camp.

"We have sent for Sleeping Bear," the translator said.

A large yellow grasshopper lighted on Slocum's shoulder. He never brushed him off, merely nodded that he had
heard the man's explanation for the boy's departure. Then,
with steel springs, the yellowish-colored insect popped up,
struck the underside of his hat brim, recovered on his vest
and then flew off into the sage. Slocum shifted his weight
in the saddle, still holding the rifle on his knees with the
fluttering flag. No doubt this would be a long day.

The bucks said little as if their part of this deal was over.
Winchester rifles across their brown knees, they sat and
waited. One leaned out and spoke to the translator, who in
turn spoke to Slocum.

"He wants to know why you brought the Army on us?"

Slocum shook his head. "I came for the woman on the
stage. The Army came from the north."

"We could have killed you."

With a nod, Slocum agreed, watching some magpies circle and light farther down the wash. "The Army could have snuck up and killed you in your tepee this morning, too, when the sun came up."

"No."

"Why not? I saw you drinking whiskey and stomping around your campfires last night while I lay only a few feet away. Where were your guards? Were they little boys too like those guarding the horses—and asleep too?"

The translator's chest swelled like a prairie chicken in his mating dance. He gritted his teeth together as he raised his chin to contain his anger. The others leaned forward and demanded in Sioux to know what Slocum had said to make him so mad.

At last he belted it out and then sat back, cross-armed, and glared at Slocum.

Slocum dismounted, turned his back to them and drained his bladder in the sand. The bay stomped his hind foot at a fly and then lowered his head and snored in the dust, as tired as Slocum felt at that point.

Then he heard hard-pounding hooves and a full head-dress appeared on a deep-red horse. The rider was a huge Indian and his muscular chest shone in the high sun. He reined up the sorrel on his heels and sprung off him. His moccasins making long strides, he stopped beside the seated men.

He spoke to them with angry words and they nodded that they heard him. Slocum figured he had asked them why they had not already killed this dog of a lone white man.

"They say you will shoot our horses—"

Slocum nodded to the chief. "I want the white woman from the stage."

"She is dead."

"Good, bring me her body."

"Bad business to mess with the dead."

With a glance at the sun time, Slocum nodded. "At dark the Army will shoot all of your horses."

"Who are you?" Sleeping Bear frowned in disapproval at him.

"A white man."

"I know that—what is your business here?"

"I want that woman."

Sleeping Bear looked out of patience. He shook his headdress in indignation. "I don't know why these men have not already killed you."

"Because I am the key to saving all your horses from being shot."

"Get out of here!" Sleeping Bear kicked dust at him.

Slocum nodded and took the flag off the rifle. He stuck it into the saddlebag and jammed the rifle in the scabbard. Then he stepped into the stirrup and swung aboard.

He caught the bay up short. "Why does a great chief of the Sioux lie to me?"

"Lie to you?" Sleeping Bear blinked in the too bright sun at him.

"If she was dead you would never have come and talked to me."

Sleeping Bear shook his head. "She is dead."

Looking at him eye to eye, Slocum shook his head back. "She is alive and well in your camp."

"Who are you, white man? Why did the yellow legs send you here?"

"If they kill all your horses, how far can you go? They would find you. You can't carry the lodgepoles on your back."

"We are Lakota Sioux and we will never give up any more of our land, if we have to die on it!" He pointed at the loose dirt between his feet.

"Without your horses, how many children will die? What women will die?" Slocum shook his head at him in pity and reined the bay around.

"Why is one woman so important?"

Slocum stopped, without turning, and nodded. "Because I am responsible for her being here."

Sleeping Bear said something in Sioux and Slocum figured that the chief wanted a better translation than his own. He twisted in the saddle to hear his man's words.

"Get off your horse," Sleeping Bear said in disgusted surrender. "I will send a boy after her."

Slocum turned the bay around and stepped down. He reached into the saddlebags and drew out some jerky. Saliva flowed into his dry mouth while Sleeping Bear told his man what to do. He began to chew on the peppery, hard, dried meat.

When the boy rode out, Sleeping Bear came over and stopped a few feet from him. He nodded his head and folded his arms over his chest.

"You are a strange white man. You gambled your life coming here."

Wallowing the jerky around to his molars with his tongue, he nodded. "I wanted her to go home to her people."

"Not many men would try such a thing."

Slocum shrugged and took down the canteen. He popped out the cork to take a drink and wash down the chewed-up jerky. Resting the container wrapped in old blanket material on the seat, he swallowed and nodded. "Not many men are such fools."

Sleeping Bear dismissed that with a wave of his hand. "If you had not come—perhaps the Army would have attacked us in camp."

"Maybe."

"No." Sleeping Bear shook his headdress feathers. "I

know the White Buffalo Goddess sent you. If the Army will let us keep our weapons and not kill any of our horses, we will go with them."

"How will they know you will not turn and kill them on the way?"

"How will we know that they won't do the same to us?"

"It's a long ways to Fort Robinson."

"I have been there." Sleeping Bear bobbed his head and the wind ruffled the many eagle feathers in his bonnet.

"I will speak to the leader and see if he will allow you all the horses."

"I would repay you."

"The woman's return is enough."

"Where is your land?"

Slocum wet his dry lips. "I have no land. It is where the sun shines on me."

"I should have known. A man with no land has nothing to lose, does he?"

"Not much."

A half hour had passed when Slocum looked up to see the youth returning, leading a woman in a fringed buckskin dress on a painted pony coming off the hillside. He could see the strain in her face and the dull look in her eyes when she drew closer.

Sleeping Bear went and took the reins from the boy. He came leading her and handed the reins over to Slocum. "For all of our horses to ride to this place you speak of—Robinson."

Slocum nodded that he understood the deal. "I'll see what I can do."

"We will wait for your answer."

He nodded and then looked at her. She never flickered an eyelash, so he turned, leading her animal, and started toward the bay. "Let's go home, Judy."

17

"You promised him what?" the wide-eyed lieutenant demanded.

"I told him if he came in peacefully, you'd not shoot any of his horses and you'd guide him to Fort Robinson to surrender."

"You know how far away that is?"

"I know it's a ways."

"A ways? Hell, it must be hundreds of miles."

"Listen, I didn't get killed and you didn't either. Here's a man with fifty or more warriors, plus all the women and children, willing to go in. What's best? Have war or take him there?"

"My orders are to—"

"Shoot the horses. But if Sleeping Bear gives up and goes to the fort, maybe some of the others will too without a fight."

"So I get to take fifty armed bucks to Fort Robinson and risk getting my men killed in the process."

Slocum looked off across the sagebrush. "I don't blame him for wanting to keep his arms. There's plenty of crazy civilians that would love to kill every Indian in sight and might try on the way there."

"I'll have to send word to my commander before I agree to anything."

"Good, maybe he can see the deal will work."

Deering shook his head in disbelief. "It's crazy."

"No, it isn't. We can all die out here or some of us can die. I'd rather live and let live."

"How's she?"

Slocum nodded, recalling his time spent comforting her. "She'll recover. She's from tough stock. It'll take time."

"I imagine so. Sergeant send me a messenger."

"Aye, sir." The noncom took off in long strides.

"We won't have word for several days."

Slocum understood. "I'd better go tell Sleeping Bear to sit tight."

"My God, man, you must need some sleep. You've been up for days now."

"I'll do that later. See to the woman while I'm gone."

Deering agreed, standing rigid in the morning sunlight.

Slocum managed to mount his horse and nodded grimly at the officer. "I'll be back. You seen the guy rode in with me—Hash?"

"He said he would take those stage-line horses back to Deadwood while you were so busy. Spoke about getting the reward for them and splitting it with you later."

That no good sumbitch. He'd left with the damn gold from the stage. There'd be no split. There was no time for Slocum to worry about the double-crossing Hash—he had bigger fish to fry out there with the Sioux. He'd catch him later.

Hours later, Slocum's eye sockets were as dry as a long-dead cow's bones when he arrived at the Sioux camp on the Powder. Dark eyes suspiciously followed him as he rode up through their village. He dismounted heavily at

Bear's lodge and the head man swept outside with a trade blanket wrapped around his waist.

"He has sent word to his chief about what he can do." Slocum looked at the man out of his right eye, trying to shake the fatigue weighing him down.

Bear nodded that he understood the meaning of his words. "You have ridden many miles. Do you wish to sleep for a while in my lodge?"

"I damn sure would like to sleep somewhere."

In minutes, he was on a pallet inside the tall tepee and sound asleep.

He awoke. The only light in the room was the low fire and the flames' reflection made the young woman's face a bright copper color as she knelt on the other side. She gathered her leather dress and came over when he sat up.

"You eat?"

"I could eat." He nodded his head that he would. Anything but dog, knowing full well the Sioux considered the meat a delicacy.

In response to his reactions, she ducked and went outside. Soon she returned with a bark platter heaped high with fresh-cooked buffalo ribs and set them before him.

"Thanks." His mouth filled with saliva at the prospect. In his effort to fill his hollow stomach, he cleaned white bone after bone. Then, at last, he wiped his mouth on his kerchief and accepted the tea she offered him. He was undecided about the source, but could taste that it was honey sweetened. He gave her a wide smile of approval.

"You are awake," Sleeping Bear said, coming inside. He took a place on the ground and sat cross-legged. "Who is this chief out there?" He swung his head with a toss of his braids toward the Army's position.

"Lieutenant Deering. Good man, young, but he's all

right. Has some good—" He sought the words that Sleeping Bear would understand. "He has some wise counsels."

"You know some of my men wish to leave here and join the others. They think I am foolish."

"The white man's clock ticks away the days that they will put up with hostiles."

Sleeping Bear nodded. "And the buffalo are like the fingers on my hand. Once I could not count them."

Slocum understood what he meant. He'd not passed any number of them any time coming across the vastness to get there.

"The loss of the buffalo will mean the end to my people."

"Perhaps there will be new days."

"No, the days ahead for my people will be without sunshine or rain. Some will choose to die rather than live in such a dim world. Others will submit."

"What about you?"

"I cry for the little ones. That is why I will go to Robinson if he will agree to the terms. I don't want them to suffer. The bucks can go join Sitting Bull or Crazy Horse, I don't care. This winter the children will be the ones to cry with empty bellies."

"I think that his chiefs will let him take you there."

"You are a strange man. You say you have no country you belong in, yet you come to me in the face of death with no fear."

"You understand loyalty?"

"Loyalty?"

"I pledge to you."

"Maybe I understand."

"I am loyal to my friends."

Sleeping Bear nodded. "I understand. You must stay for the dances tonight."

His eyes closed, Slocum shook his head. "I'd only make

some of the men uncomfortable. I see it in their eyes. I will return when I know the answer."

"You will return even if the answer is no," Sleeping Bear said and rose.

"Even if the answer is no."

Slocum arrived at the Army's camp after dark. He found Deering in his tent and sat down on a canvas camp stool. The man nodded and held up a hand while he signed some papers in the yellow light of his candle reflector.

"My orders are to take those people to Fort Robinson," Deering said, sitting in the straight-backed chair behind the small folding desk.

Slocum nodded.

"I cannot guarantee what the commander there will do about his stock."

"Good, we can cross that bridge when we get there."

"Colonel Wright has offered you scout pay to go along with and help the outfit, since you know so much about them and seem to be able to deal with them."

"John Wright?"

"That's him."

"Good man, I knew him in Kansas when he was captain."

"Yes, he said so. He sent his regards and thanks too."

"Tell the colonel I'll go along with your outfit."

The relieved face on the young officer broke into a smile. "Good. When can they leave?"

"I would suspect in two days."

"I'm going to be on my guard, Slocum. I don't intend for this to be a trap for them to kill my men."

With his palm, Slocum scrubbed the itchy side of his face. "Sleeping Bear is worried about the children."

"What does that mean?"

Slocum rose to his feet. He wanted to find her, to be certain she was all right and to get something to eat.

"Lieutenant, he's as worried as you are about this trip and what will happen to his people at Fort Robinson too."

"I think I understand. Will all of his people come in?"

With a shake of Slocum's head, he stretched his stiff arms over his hat. "No, some have already left, to join the hostiles I am certain."

"You will make arrangements to start the move?"

"I'll go back in the morning and get them started. I want a noncom that he can trust to go with me."

Deering frowned at his request.

"He respects real men. If you send your best then he will know you are a man of your word and things will go better."

"Sergeant O'Day will go with you."

"I hear you. Thanks." And Slocum left the officer's tent. The road to Robinson would be a long one. He hoped the sun would shine and it would rain some on them too.

18

Slocum squatted on his boot heels, grateful for the plate of food and for being in Judy's company. She sat on the ground wrapped in a clean blanket. Orange flames from the fire shone on the hollowness in her look that knifed him in the gut.

"I hate that Steven's still with those outlaws—I haven't done anything about it . . ."

"Well, maybe it wasn't meant to be. What I mean—" He used his empty fork to point off in the night. "He's got lots of things going against him. He's part of that gang."

"I guess, but I can hardly believe that. My father is a bitter man, but he must have suspected that when he wouldn't send his ransom."

Slocum nodded and forked in more of the antelope meat and potatoes the army cook had provided him with. "You're upset about the kidnapping and your treatment. That too will pass."

She hugged the blanket closer. "I hope so."

"I'll take you home after we get them to Robinson."

"I can take a stage by myself from there."

He shook his head and swallowed. "No, I'll see you home."

"So I can be some old spinster and rock in my chair and remember being abducted by Indians."

"You need a husband."

"Oh, yes. And what do you propose to do about it?"

"I'll have to work on it."

"Oh sure, damaged goods. What man would want me?"

"You don't tell them they'd never know." He considered the last of the food on his tin plate.

She dropped her chin and shook her head. "I would."

"You don't tell them." He scraped up the last juices with the crust of bread. "They'll be so dazzled they'll never know nothing but how good it was."

For the first time she smiled at him. "I guess you know more about men than I do."

"I damn sure do." He paused, considering what to do next. "That food was so good I'm getting me some more. Sit right there."

She sighed. "I'm not going anywhere."

He flashed a grin at her first flicker of response. "That a girl." Then he struggled to his feet with the plate in hand. Damn, every muscle in his body ached. And he still had Hash to think about—Hash, who had taken the stage coach loot and a big powder. Nothing he could do about that for the moment—and that would only give him a bigger head start.

After he finished eating, they went off by themselves out in the sagebrush. He found a draw of soft green grass, spread his ground cloth down and they wrapped themselves in two blankets. Fully clothed, she snuggled her ripe body to his and he awoke twice in the night with her kicking her legs like a paddle wheel as if to somehow escape.

But she never awoke. He shifted a stiff arm, cuddled her close and went back to sleep.

A predawn light was spreading light across the hills to the east when he awoke and eased himself up. Sitting on his butt he pulled on his run-over boots.

"You leaving?" she asked in a sleep-hoarse voice.

"Got to go back and tell Sleeping Bear we've got a deal."

She sat up and rubbed her eyes with her fists. "I slept for the first time last night. When will you be back?"

"Two days. Unless something happens. But I plan to re join you then."

She rose, straightened her skirt and nodded. "Be careful."

"I will. The Army will watch out for you."

"Oh, they're very nice."

"Good. In two days."

She dropped her face. "I almost forgot it all."

"Work on it."

They rolled up his bedroll and headed back for camp. When they crossed the ridge he could see the soldiers were already busy in camp.

The officer took off his hat and nodded to her. "Good morning."

"I leave her in your care," Slocum said.

"She will be safe."

"Who rides with me?"

"Sergeant O'Day. Best fist-fighter in the outfit."

Slocum laughed. "He won't have to fight."

"No, but he's a hard man to deny and straight as an arrow."

"Good, the Sioux appreciate fighting men."

"Had breakfast yet?"

"No but we'll fall in line."

"No reason for that. Corporal will have some food and

coffee sent over for our guests. Ma'am, you will have my tent from now on."

"But—but you will need it."

"No, I can do my business out under these Wyoming skies."

"Thank you," she said and Slocum would have thought she blushed some under the officer's gaze.

Judy would make it.

After their breakfast and parting with her, he and the red-faced bull of a sergeant, Shawn O'Day, rode for the hostiles' camp.

"How long have you been in the Army?" Slocum asked as they trotted their horses in the coolness of the morning.

"Twenty years. Since I came over from emerald sod, lad."

"Not much out here looks like that," Slocum said.

"Aye, but I ain't missed many meals since joining this man's Army. Oh, it was tough in the war and sometimes out here. When it was the worst I wished I'd become a shoe cobbler like me pappy wanted me to be, but aye that weren't for the likes of me."

Slocum nodded. They rode on.

Late afternoon they reached the heights that would lead them to the Powder River bottoms, a jumble of grassy, sagebrush folded hills that stair-stepped down to the river. So that Sleeping Bear had not changed his mind; the notion niggled him as he made out some fine wisps of smoke. The Sioux were still there, or at least part of them were, at the camp.

Dogs barked and several grown-ups raised their brown eyes to suspiciously scan them. Small children in shirts with bare brown butts cautiously trailed him and O'Day. But they scattered when Slocum twisted in the saddle and dared to smile at them.

Sleeping Bear came out of his tent with a blanket

around his waist and his great brown chest covered with a bone-pipe vest. He wore no headdress but his black hair, in thick braids, shone with bear grease.

"Who is this man?" Sleeping Bear motioned toward the noncom.

"He is a chief from the Army's camp. Sergeant O'Day. The blue legs listen to this man and he is a fierce fighter."

Sleeping Bear nodded. "Looks plenty damn tough. Come, we have tea and talk more about trip."

"He don't mean India kind of tea," Slocum warned the sergeant as he ducked over to go into the tepee.

"Good, I prefer coffee meself." Then O'Day removed his hat and went on inside.

The sides were raised up a foot and a half all around so the afternoon wind ventilated the structure and let light inside the tepee. A young woman served them a drink in small cups that had a waft of sage and berries. O'Day took a sip and nodded his approval.

Bear showed them places to sit around the small fire. Then he sat down and looked at both men. "My women want to gather some chokecherries on the way. There will be some to collect."

O'Day frowned and waited for an answer from Slocum.

"I understand your concern for food for the coming winter, but we must get there."

"They will work fast," Bear promised.

O'Day nodded and said in approval, "Good."

"If we find some buffalo on the way, can we kill them?" Sleeping Bear asked.

"Yes" Slocum agreed. "But you can only leave a few squaws behind to jerk them."

O'Day agreed to that.

"We can leave in three days if you bring back the horses."

"How many have gone to join Sitting Bull and the others?" Slocum asked with dread.

"Some."

"How many handsful?" Slocum asked, knowing the question was bugging O'Day too. If a majority of the men had run off and there were only women left behind, he doubted the Army would like the transfer.

Bear held up eight fingers. "My son is one. Youth can afford to be stubborn and know more than their elders."

"You know the soldiers are told to either tell them to go back or fight them, whatever they want to do."

"And to kill the horses."

O'Day nodded grimly. "The excess ones."

"What is excess?" Sleeping Bear asked with a frown.

"Ones you don't need to pack or ride," Slocum said.

"But what if one goes lame or dies or runs away."

Slocum shrugged. He didn't always have answers for Indians that questioned the white man's ways or his rules. "They fear too many horses make the Sioux too easy to run away or raid."

Sleeping Bear nodded, then he spoke. "But my people have no cows, we have no money—horses are our only wealth."

"But it is the horse that makes the warrior," O'Day said.

"I can see that Slocum has done my people a favor to make such deal with your men." Bear nodded toward the noncom. "We will meet you east of here where the Wild Horse Creek comes through the hills if you will bring the rest of our horses back to us. There is water enough there for our stock and then we can head for Fort Robinson."

"Good. We'll have the horses back to you in two days," O'Day said.

19

"Bull Elk is not with them?" Judy asked in a whisper.

With a concerned frown, Slocum shook his head. "Why?"

"He's their war chief. He's the one that—kept me. I can't believe he's not around the camp."

"I guess he went to join the others up in the Bozeman Trail Country." He hugged her in the starlight. No telling where Bull Elk was at. Just so that he wasn't hiding out in the sagebrush planning an uprising on the trip to Fort Robinson. The other thing niggling him—he had no more word of Charlie Hash and the loot's whereabouts. He'd been so fascinated with the notion about all the fancy pussy that gold would buy, he might be spending it on that purpose at that very moment.

"What happens next?" she asked.

"We take the horses back to the Sioux in the morning and start for Robinson."

"You be careful. Bull Elk is treacherous."

He nodded that he'd heard her and listened to a couple of coyotes howling off in the night. Her firm body pressed against his. He wondered—but not for long.

Her hard nipples soon knifed through his shirt as she pressed her body to his. He looked down into her shadowy face, then he dropped his mouth to hers. Honey spilled from her lips when he tasted them and he knew the real Judy was back.

They hurried off to the draw where they quickly spread out his bedroll. He checked around under the dim starlight as he toed off his boots to be certain they were alone. She already had the front buttons undone on her blouse and her breasts spilled out in the dull silver light. They shook with their firmness as she stripped off the shirt. Then, with a mischievous grin at him, she undid the skirt's ties at her waist and began to shed it.

Beside her on the blankets the day's dying heat swept over their bare skin in small breaths of wind. His calloused palm slid over her smooth skin, exploring and rubbing. Their mouths sought great things. Her hot tongue, like a branding iron, searched his mouth, his fingers molding the rock hard breasts and his thumb teasing the pointed nipples.

Her fingers played over the corduroy muscles of his stomach. Then she reached deeper and combed through his pubic hair, the tips of her fingers tracing over his top of his half-erect dick. Her mouth pressed hard to his, she raised up to kiss him harder and clutched his shaft in her fist so hard he feared she might squeeze it off.

There was nothing he could do but follow her persistent tugging and roll over between her raised legs. She stuffed him into her wet gates and threw her head back at his entry. The cry from her throat was loud and filled with abandonment. He wondered who besides the coyotes had heard her, but he drove his shaft deep into her and she raised her hips for more.

"Oh, Gawd—yes," she moaned and her hands pulled him harder down on top of her.

Then the walls began to swell and tightened on his

aching dick. The effort to drive his engorged shaft into her grew harder and harder. A force was pulling—no grabbing at the skin-tight head when he was to the very depth of her. Her heels locked behind his knees and she hunched herself to his every move into her.

Then she began to whisper. "Yes—yes—" in a cadence with his efforts and he knew they both would soon explode or faint from the effort. Their ragged breathing sounded like a wind-broke horse who'd been ran for miles.

Then he felt the stirring in his scrotum and arrows shot into his butt. The explosion was coming and he drove his throbbing sword hard into her. She held her breath and strained with gritted teeth. One second passed, two seconds passed. He pushed so hard his efforts shut off his hearing—then he felt the volcano exploding out the head of his dick. Not once but like repeated cannon fire; when he slumped for a moment, something squeezed both testicles and another round shot out of the aching head.

Dizzy from his efforts, he braced himself with stiff arms above her. His dick still drove full-tilt into her and the third barrage, less violent than the others, went off with a depleting finale.

He inhaled a heady nose full of the sage's pungent aroma. *Whew.*

Up before dawn, he joined Sergeant O'Day and the six troopers assigned to drive the Sioux horse herd back to them. Earlier in the night, Judy had gone back to the tent that the lieutenant had so graciously given her for her own use. After their tender parting Slocum found a few hours of sleep. But his eyes still felt like sand holes and his back ached every time he moved in the saddle. He needed someone to hold the muscles tight or together. He tried to shake all the numbness from his mind but neither the Army's bitter coffee nor the dull sunup helped his condition—he'd simply have to live with his hangover. He booted the roan after a straggler.

The horses acted like they knew the way and moved briskly westward in a mass. All the help made the job even easier. O'Day reined up beside him on a rise and nodded in approval.

"We should be there by early afternoon?"

"Should," Slocum said, stretching his tender back muscles and then settling into the saddle, clasping the reins and the horn in his hand. It was hard to forget Judy's ripe body and think about the things ahead—what he really needed to do. And she kept talking about Bull Elk being the war chief? He wished his mind would clear and he could think. Too damn hungover and pussy-whipped to do much of anything, he decided, and managed to make small talk with O'Day. But only with an extreme effort.

The hours drug on. Dust from the hundreds of hooves, and the day's rising heat, made his mind duller by the passing hour. There had to be an answer to all the things spinning through his mind. Get the Sioux to Fort Robinson. Find Hash before he spent all the loot and get Judy home—that left her brother in the throes of the gun sellers and God only knew what else. He booted the roan after another bunch-quitter.

They arrived at Horse Creek and were greeted by several tribal members on horseback, excited about their return. Even Sleeping Bear rode out and spoke to him and O'Day.

"We killed three buffalo, so tell your men to come to our camp," Bear told the noncom.

O'Day agreed and rode off to talk to his men who were off their horses and washing their faces at the creek.

"You have returned," Sleeping Bear said to Slocum.

Slocum nodded. "Where is Bull Elk?"

"Gone with the others who went to join Crazy Horse."

"He's not out there with the coyotes?" Slocum made a sweeping gesture with his arm.

"No, he was mad when I took the white woman from him. He and a handful have gone to join the wild ones."

Slocum nodded. He would have been mad too—if someone had taken her away from him. Still, he felt there was something Sleeping Bear wasn't telling him.

"Will he come back for his horses?"

Sleeping Bear raised his face toward the sky and then shook his head. "I don't know."

"You told me they are his only wealth. Would he go to join Crazy Horse without his wealth?"

"Or without his white slave?"

Oh, shit. Slocum's heart sunk at the chief's words. It was something he had never thought about—Bull Elk coming back for her. He felt the toe of a flying boot punch his belly and his mind at once was clearer than it had been all day.

"Loan me your best horse. I want to go to her."

Sleeping Bear acknowledged his request and shouted to a nearby boy herder on horseback. The youth's copper face glowed in the bloody sunset at being asked. He grinned big and nodded with a firmness of "I will get that one for you."

His fingers tore at the latigo straps as he hurried to strip the saddle off the roan and then piled it on the ground. He raised up, looking for the boy to be returning. If only— damn. Why had he not put that together? Filled with impatience, he shook his head and glanced over as Sleeping Bear joined him.

"Men grow desperate when things they plan do not happen."

"You think Bull Elk will do something desperate?"

His head bobbed slow-like—enough to shake the thick

braids on his broad shoulders. "When a man's pride is at stake, he will do many things good sense would never let him do."

"No horses, no slave."

"Such as it is."

The boy came flying in, leading a high-headed stallion, a black piebald who danced on his toes and shrill-whistled through his nostrils. Slocum tossed the blankets on the horse's back while Sleeping Bear held his head. Then the saddle went on and the big horse shied despite Slocum's coaxing. In spite of his movements to avoid him, Slocum followed him and soon cinched up the girths. When the saddling suited him Slocum took the reins of his bridle, which Bear had slipped in the stud's mouth.

"Be careful, my friend, he's a tough adversary."

Slocum moved to the right side and slipped onto the stallion's back from there. In his seat he checked the prancing animal.

A broad grin of approval spread over Sleeping Bear's face. "Ride back to us."

"When I can. Tell O'Day where I've gone." The noncom and his men were already out of sight in the camp, collecting their meal. He put his heels to the stallion and flew toward the darkening eastern horizon.

A powerful animal, the piebald sped away in easy flight. Slocum pulled down his hat by the brim out of habit when the headband threatened to loosen on his head. The long night stretched behind him. The route would be uphill for several miles, climbing out of the tributary of the Powder. They reached the top of the first grade when the quarter moon rose in the east. Still miles lay between him and her. He urged the big horse on. Unshod hooves drummed a song in the night. An urgent one for him.

20

"Halt!" a guard challenged him in the darkness.

"Slocum," he shouted and drew up the hard-breathing horse, grateful he had managed to return so easily to the camp.

"What brings you back in such a rush?" the soldier asked, coming forward, carrying his carbine in front of his chest.

"Is the woman in camp?"

"I guess so. She's in the lieutenant's tent—I think."

Slocum nodded. He hoped the man knew the facts about it. The guard nodded back to him, then sent the stomping horse on. He'd better go and check for himself.

At the tent he bounded out of the saddle and pulled back the tent flap. Reflection from the campfire shone on Judy's sleeping face and he felt relieved. The strength drained from his legs when he let go of the canvas flap and it fell shut.

"What in the hell are you back for?"

Slocum turned and faced the young officer knifing in his shirttail as he huriedly crossed the camp. Then something moved in the corner of his eye—and Slocum dove and tackled him.

"What the hell—"

An arrow clattered across the ground beyond them. Another split the night air and struck the tent side with a thud, quivering and then falling to the ground.

"Sergeant, sound the alarm. We're under attack." By then both he and Slocum were on their bellies, holding handguns in their fists and looking hard into the night for the unseen enemy.

"How the hell did you know?" Deering demanded.

"I was playing on the odds."

In minutes, the entire camp was awake, men smothering the complaining voices of their comrades. The awareness of the attackers was being taken seriously as they kept low and searched for the source in the inky night.

"Is it over?" Deering rolled over on his back to search behind them for any sight of the arrow shooter.

Slocum whispered, "No. It's only begun."

"You certain?"

"He'll come back for her, if he don't succeed this time."

"I can't blame him—"

"I better get her to stay down. I think she's stirring in all this."

"Yes, do that. Keller, see if you can get any idea about where they are or went."

"Yes, sir."

When Slocum parted the flap back, the faint light of the fire shone on a dark face and bulky form standing over her. His heart stopped and he shoved the .45 ahead in one cocking, trigger-pulling thrust. The smoke pillowed and he heard her cry. He drove forward and felt a hard blow to his head. The force of the hit dropped him to his knees and the world went black.

In moments, he could hear her talking in his ear. ". . . you all right?"

"How the hell did he get away?" Deering was asking outside.

"Bull Elk?" Slocum whispered, holding his sore head in both hands.

"Yes—I woke up and saw his face. Then I screamed and you came inside."

"You shoot him?" Lieutenant Deering asked from the open flap.

Slocum rolled over and sat on his butt with his back to the cot. "I may have creased him."

"You all right, miss?"

"Sure. How bad did he hit you over the head?" She tried to examine Slocum's scalp. He could feel her trembling fingers parting his hair, looking for a wound.

"I'll live." He shared a private reassuring look at her before he turned to the lieutenant. "How about your sentries?"

"Sergeant Malloy has gone to check on them. How many men were with him, do you think?"

Slocum shook his head. "I have no idea, but maybe he came in alone to sneak close enough to get her."

Deering lit a small candle reflector lamp. "Bold bastard—sorry, miss, for my language, but I'm upset."

"He's no longer part of Sleeping Bear's bunch," Slocum said.

"I certainly hope not. We have weeks of being close to them on this odyssey you have me on."

"Come daylight, I'll see where he went."

"I think we better plan on taking him into custody or shooting him before we go a mile with that bunch of Sioux."

Slocum understood the man's concern, but gathering Bull Elk would not be easy. He was like the shadows on the

canvas tent-side as Slocum hugged Judy's shoulders and
tried to comfort her.

"You be all right?"

"Fine, but be careful."

He promised her he would and went outside. Malloy
was back with a wounded sentry. The man's condition
looked minor but, nonetheless, Bull Elk had breached their
security.

In the starlight, Slocum spotted Kellar returning by the
outline of the man's hat brim—a wide, straw one.

"Any sign?" Slocum squatted down, hoping the scout
would do the same and they could palaver about the war
chief.

"I think he had a horse in a nearby wash. Must have
been alone."

Slocum nodded then looked off at the morning star,
blinking like a large diamond in the dark sky. "He has several young bucks with him, I figure. Some of those Hash
and I tied up I have never seen again in Sleeping Bear's
camp. There's no doubt they're with Bull Elk."

"What do we do?"

"Deering wants Bull Elk captured or killed before he
joins the rest of the Sioux for the trip to Robinson."

"Man, that might be tough."

"I know, unless . . ."

"You got a plan?"

"They were going to use the stage loot to buy guns from
Cunningham out of Deadwood. If we could be at that
meeting we might could get him."

"They've still got the loot?"

"No, but Cunningham don't know that."

"So they might try to bluff him out of them guns."

"Ain't much honor among that kind." Slocum shifted
his weight to the other leg.

"Where're they going to meet him?"

"That I don't know but maybe I can find out."

"How?"

"They might have said something around Judy. I'll try asking her first."

"What if she don't know?"

"Then I'll ask Sleeping Bear."

"Will he tell you anything?"

Slocum nodded. "Yes, I think he would."

"We ain't got much time." Keller pushed off the ground with his rifle butt for a brace. "I hate that that sumbitch got into this camp. That'll unnerve them green troopers."

"It damn sure ain't your fault."

Keller rose. "Yeah, I'm making it mine. Let's get some grub—they've got some cooking—and see if she knows anything."

Slocum found her in the tent, sitting in the middle of the cot, wrapped in a blanket against the predawn coolness.

"Couldn't go back to sleep?"

"No." She shook her head. "I'd damn near forgot him."

"Sorry, I had no idea what he planned."

She sighed aloud. "I guess there is no getting away from him."

"He won't bother you again."

She shrugged and dropped her chin.

"Did you ever hear them talk about buying guns?"

"Why? You said that Steven was involved in that business."

Slocum squatted down on his heels and then he nodded. "He's part of it. But I need to know where Bull Elk planned to meet them to buy the guns."

"I can't help you. They spoke in Sioux."

"I think Keller and I are going to try to track him. You

stay with Deering. You'll be safe. No one will sneak in again. The Army will be ready the next time."

"If I'd never left Kansas—"

"If you'd never left Kansas you'd have been upset at not knowing, even if what you know isn't any damn good."

She looked to the tent's peak for help. Then she agreed and smiled. "Say that again."

"I can't."

They both laughed. He rose, ducking under the canvas ceiling, and started outside. "I better get some grub."

"Be careful," she said softly and he gave her a reasuring nod.

21

Keller grasped his rifle's muzzle in both hands and they both stood staring across the tumultuous ocean of purple sage and brown grass toward a pine-fringed ridge.

"If you were an Injun and were meeting a gun trader, that ridge might be the best place for cover and being close to the road the military used."

"Sounds good, and since he's been joined by several bucks, a few at a time—it makes sense," Slocum said, going for the brass telescope from his saddlebags.

"Yeah, they ain't having no Injun picnic up here."

"They also have not stopped and killed any of the scattered buffalos they've passed. That would leave more sign that they were here, finding a carcass or two."

"You figure they're that smart?" Keller asked.

Using the telescope to scan the ridge, Slocum said, "Yes. Don't ever underestimate the enemy. He's formidable."

"See anything?"

"Yeah, he left a white wing, tied high up in a pine tree, to mark something. I can see it fluttering in the wind."

"Huh? Why do that?"

"A sign to either more of his men or to Cunningham to come in."

"Hell, I would never have thought about that. How're we going to get closer?"

"Dark. Then we can sneak up and see what's going on."

"Two of us—" Keller went to shaking his head in strong disapproval. "A dozen of them and we're going to get our asses shot off."

"I don't aim to let that happen."

"Well, I want to see it first."

Slocum closed the telescope. "See you then."

"What are you going to do?"

"Go find me a place to hide and sleep till dark anyway."

Keller gave a last look at the ridge. "Wished I knew for sure why they used a white wing up there."

Slocum found a cedar bush to crawl under and lay out his bedroll. He hobbled the horse he'd drawn from the military, not needing a stallion to creep up and spy on some renegades that would easily be spooked by anything. The long-legged bay was sound and a little gaunt but he'd eat every chance he got—a good hustler was important in a western horse. So, hoping for more night wind to cool things, Slocum went to sleep.

He awoke to someone hissing for him. Propped up on his belly, his sleep-gritted eyes caught sight of Keller bounding off the sagebrush hillside on the run.

"They're all there. The wagons're there now too."

"Good, how many toughs came with the wagons?"

"Why, shit fire! I never thought about more—how we going to handle all of them?"

"I ain't too certain, but we can't let them bucks get off with a bunch of rifles."

"How're they buying them, anyway, if that guy Hash

has all their money?" Keller squatted down while Slocum rolled up his bedding and tied it.

"Guess they had more or they're bluffing Cunningham into the fact they have any at all."

Keller agreed with solemn nod. "How many guns they got over there?

"Couple of cases and ammo. They had more than that they'd draw too much suspicion. Folks recognize shipments of rifles, know the markings on the wooden crates and the size. That would send tongues wagging. Might even get you a vigilante hanging too. They're selling them some, but it ain't no wagonload of guns."

"What we going to do about it?"

"Not much till dark. The lieutenant is too busy to come help us and would never get here in time. So it's up to you and me. And we may not get a damn thing done."

"We got to wait around all day?" Keller asked, looking in disgust at Slocum.

"I'd say that we better. We ride up there now they'd pick us off like pigeons."

"Oh, hell, I know that. I'm used to riding back and getting the Army."

"Well, we're the Army."

Keller dropped to his butt and shook his head. "Yeah and there's only two of us again."

The day crawled by and the distant pop of rifles they could hear meant to Slocum that the renegades were armed with repeaters. Damn. He wondered if Judy's brother Steven was over there. He expected him to be. No telling. After dark maybe they could sneak up on the camp and learn something.

"The wagons ain't leaving?" Keller asked, returning from observing them.

"I thought they'd be gone by now. It may be over Bull Elk not having the money."

"What'll they do?"

"Keller, if I knew that I wouldn't be waiting till dark to try and learn something."

"Yeah, you got a point."

Sundown came slowly, dripping bloodred flames on the western sky, the sun finally dropping below the horizon. A coyote came out and yipped at the quarter moon rising in the northeast. The two set out on foot for the pine ridge.

A good-size fire was blazing up and someone was beating on a drum. Slocum nodded in approval. They were celebrating and would probably dance, a sign that they'd be less on guard. They circled in and came from the north. Past the sleeping horse in a picket line, they held their breath while a drunk buck went by them, mumbling to himself. When he was gone they moved on. Taking cover and being cautious, they advanced on the two wagons outlined by the blaze.

Slocum could see when he was belly down under the first wagon that the bucks were in a circle. The orange flames reflected off their copper faces. Many held new Winchesters, still shiny with packing grease. They looked well supplied with whiskey crocks, passing them around and fixing to have themselves a real party.

Where were the white men? No sign of them out there. Then he looked to his right beyond the wagon and saw the prone ivory bodies—stripped of their clothing. They had captured the gun-sellers, killed them, probably after an all night torture party, and took all their clothing.

"Holy shit," Keller said, pointing his finger at the corpses.

"Yes," Slocum whispered.

"What now?"

"Let them get drunk and we'll steal their horses. Afoot, even armed, they won't get far." He gave a head toss for them to back out from under the wagon. No need in being discovered before they could execute his plan.

Bent over, they hurried through the night toward the back of the camp and soon were past the horses in the cedar brush. Slocum went to breathing easier as they squatted down to wait and study the camp's activity from a distance.

"Who's that?" Keller hissed at him.

Someone hatless was sneaking up on the camp. In the darkness there was no way to tell, but whoever it was kept stopping and searching around. Not Indian-like, Slocum decided. He must be a survivor that got away.

"We sure can't let him steal a horse yet," Slocum said in Keller's ear. "That would have the Indians upset and we'd never get to take all of them with us."

Keller agreed and both of them started after the unknown one. Soon they were right behind him. Keller tackled him and Slocum clamped his hand over the man's mouth.

"Be quiet," Slocum said in his ear. The man nodded and, slow-like, Slocum let his hand off.

"How many are you?" the breathless youth asked in bewilderment.

"Two."

"Two!"

"Hush. We can't let you steal a horse yet." Slocum realized that their prisoner was her brother Steven.

He sat on his butt, trembling all over. "I got to get out of here. How I managed to get away last night I don't know but I've got to get away."

"We'll take you when we leave. But we want them on foot."

"They tortured and killed the others—I heard them screaming for help from where I was hiding in the brush last night."

"Who did they get?"

"Cunningham, Wolf and Rader."

"Them other two work for Cunningham?"

"Yeah."

"How many guns did he bring?"

"Twenty-four."

"Lots of ammo?"

"Yeah."

"Bull Elk have any money?"

"No. He said he would get it, then things turned nasty. At the time, I was in the brush taking a crap. I had a belly-ache—saved my life." Steven drew a deep breath up his nose and hugged his arms to control the shaking.

"Rest easy, we'll be moving soon."

"Yeah—thanks."

"How we going to get them? I mean the Army?" Keller asked.

"Send some men over and capture them."

"They'll be armed and sure to be mad as hornets."

"Steven, is the ammo in the wagons?"

"Yeah, the back one. Why?"

Slocum shared a look in the darkness with Keller, who nodded. "One of us needs to get in that wagon and be sure it burns."

"Rifles without ammo ain't worth much," Keller said.

"You two get these horses ready to drive. I'll set the wagon on fire and come on the run."

"That's risky."

Slocum agreed and fingered the torpedo-headed matches in his vest pocket. He'd need a real fire and fast.

With a nod of agreement with Keller, Slocum set out for the back of the wagon.

Once he was forced to drop behind a barrel, but the drunk Indian went off the other way, to his relief. Then, in a burst of speed, he reached the back of the rig, had his knee on the wagon floor and was quickly under the canvas.

Fuel—the ammo boxes looked secure enough. But a smile came to his face: there were several small kegs of black powder. Indians still had muzzle-loaders and needed it. He drew his Colt and used it to crack the board cover when the noisy dancers were at a peak in their chanting. He opened another and spread the strong-smelling granules all over the ammo boxes, then made a track of it to the rear. There would not be much time between his lighting the powder and a hell of an explosion.

Checking around, he slipped out of the wagon and drew a deep breath to steady himself. One chance was all he would get to set off his surprise. The Indians at the nearby fire were whooping it up. He drew out a match, struck it and the flame about blinded him. Then he touched the fire to the powder. A small flicker, then the trail of black flared and he ran as hard as he could. Not looking back, he reached the horses when the blast went skyward. He mounted the one Keller held the reins to. In seconds they were screaming at the dull animals panicked by the blinding, ear-shattering blast.

Ponies on the move, they swept them westward under the stars, off the pine ridge toward their own camp. When Slocum looked back and saw the exploding rounds of ammo fill the night sky with more fireworks, he smiled. *Sorry, Bull Elk, you ain't using those bullets.*

22

In the early morning light, Lieutenant Deering chewed on a grass stem. He used it for a pointer too. "You mean that Bull Elk is afoot with empty rifles?"

"He don't have much ammo." Slocum shared a nod with Keller.

"How many men could capture him and his renegades?"

"A dozen good troopers."

"I need to meet Sleeping Bear and that's a third of my men. How would it look to show short that many men?"

"To capture Bull Elk might be a smooth move. Be a feather in your cap to bring him into Fort Robinson in chains, wouldn't it?"

"Would he surrender?"

Slocum looked over at Keller for his answer.

"Don't matter. Foot first or walking in chains."

"Sergeant O'Day is the toughest man I've got and the one to send back with you with the troopers. If I don't show up with him or you, Slocum, what will Sleeping Bear think?"

"Tell him what we're doing."

"I don't know. My guts tell me this is a trap."

"Your guts are lying to you."

"I hope so. What do we need to do?"

Slocum explained his and Keller's ideas on how to capture the renegades. O'Day was sent for and told the plans.
He went to pick nine good men and have them supplied for
a three-day march. Slocum left to find Judy and her brother.

Steven excused himself when he came and left them to
talk.

"I never thought I'd see him alive again," she said with
wetness gleaming on her lashes.

"He was lucky."

"Yes. He's going home with me and try to patch up with
Father."

"Reckon it will work?"

"I'll make it work."

"Good, that's what you came for."

She chewed on her lower lip. "Will you ever come by
again?"

"Can't say. Don't plan on it."

"When you get broke and need money you could wire
me."

He nodded that he heard her.

"Well I won't be leaving the Army's escort until we
reach some sort of civilization."

"I'll be in and out."

"Good—" She searched around the area outside the tent
flap to be sure she would not be heard and then smiled. "I
want to share your bedroll at least once more."

"I'll try."

"Good. Be careful out there. Bull Elk is like a badger. I
think if you back him up he'll claw you."

"I'll heed your warning."

She stepped over and hugged him. "I'm so glad you
brought him back to me."

Slocum nodded. He could only hope he'd done the right thing. Maybe the Indian deal had put the fear of God in Steven. Slocum hoped so anyway. A quick kiss and he was on his way to find O'Day and the small force of men assembling with horses to ride.

Slocum took his piebald stallion, who had to dance around and act up some after his rest. In thirty minutes they were on the move at a steady trot. Keller had set out ahead to look for them. The troopers all looked like weathered, toughened veterans and O'Day said they were the best.

By late afternoon Keller had them on the renegades' tracks headed toward the northwest. Obviously they were all on foot, for no signs of a hoof showed among the moccasin prints. So by sundown the men went into dry camp. Their horses were picketed close inside their circle to prevent any stealing and guards were posted out from the sleeping men.

Before dawn they mounted up and, with the purple sky about to turn pink, Keller spotted the band hurrying across a ridge ahead. They spread out and charged. A few shots were fired at them but the rest threw up their hands. Slocum looked for the tall Bull Elk among those bucks on the hillside surrendering. Seeing no sight of him, he drove the stallion up the steep grade and halted.

Looking across the vast rolling land he saw nothing save a small band of antelope. Where was Bull Elk? He booted the stallion downhill and dropped off a steep bank. The stud skidded on his hooves to the bottom of the draw lined with several big rock outcroppings.

Out of nowhere came a scream; then someone grabbed his arm and the lights went out.

•   •   •

Slocum spit sand and felt for the knot on his head when he came to. The ache in his temples pounded like two rocks on each side of his head, driven in by hammers.

"You all right?" Keller asked, swinging off his horse.

"Yeah, I got jumped on by Bull Elk, who was hiding down here in the rocks and he, I guess"—he squinted his eyes against the too-bright glare—"got my horse."

"You sure you're all right?"

"Head hurts, but yes, I'll live." He dragged himself to his feet. The world tilted and he used his hand on the nearby large boulder to steady himself. "Guess he hadn't been in such a rush he'd of sure killed me."

"Might have. He sure got the hell out of here fast enough."

"He's riding a damn good horse." Slocum smiled and both men laughed.

"Anyway, we got the rest of them bucks. No one hurt either. Your plan worked that good." Keller mounted up and offered him a hand.

"Hey, if we'd ever gotten Bull Elk it would have been perfect." He swung up behind the scout and, forced to sit upon the scout's bedroll, could see over his head. No sign of the war chief.

They could see the dust of Sleeping Bear's camp on the move long before they could see anything else. The brown cloud looked welcome to Slocum as they rode over a rise and surveyed the movement. They were Fort Robinson bound. Maybe after all that happened, he could go search for that sneaky Hash and see if any of the gold was left. Judy had her brother—but Slocum didn't know how dependable he'd be once the fear of his close call wore off. Perhaps when she was safely on a stage headed for Kansas he could go look for Hash.

"Heckuva bruise there," Deering said, looking closely at where Bull Elk had tried to bash in his head.

"It's still tender."

"Nineteen bucks ain't a bad roundup and twenty new Winchester rifles recovered."

"We lost four, I figure. They come a dozen to the crate. But they might have been in that explosion too—I never looked close enough."

"It's a good catch. And I'm overlooking Steven's involvement in that gun deal."

Slocum nodded. "Thanks for her. He acts changed, anyway."

Deering agreed, bent over and took a bottle of whiskey from his kit. The sunlight shone through the brown liquor and Slocum nodded in approval. A little whiskey would go just fine for him at that moment. That and two days' sleep and a belly full of food—he might consider himself alive again. His head still hurt.

The next five days were dry, dusty and blistering hot. Water for the horse herd, let alone for all the people, proved difficult. Then on the sixth they reached a stream that had to be filtered through rags to separate out the mud but it quenched everyone's thirst.

When they all laid about the camp in total exhaustion, Keller returned and told them a clear stream coming out of the Black Hills was less than three miles away. They camped on it the next day and everyone rested. The Indian women and children bathed and swam in the pretty water. Soldiers caught silver trout and cooked them on the bank. The change from their mess was a welcome relief.

That afternoon the Sioux located and shot two mature buffalos. The meat was quickly carried by travois back to camp. By evening everyone had gorged themselves on the roasted meat and lounged about, satisfied they had found heaven.

Slocum was sitting with Deering on a blanket, sharing their meal with Sleeping Bear.

"White man eat cow. Sioux eat buffalo. Not the same."

"Longhorns ain't good beef," Slocum said. Then he held up another meaty rib. "This is real good."

The three men laughed and Deering wiped his mouth on a clean kerchief before going after another rib. "I'll never be able to stand Army grub again."

"This will spoil you," Slocum agreed.

"Makes you wonder," Deering said between bites. "What's Bull Elk eating out there?"

"Ravens," Sleeping Bear said.

"In Alabama, we call them crows," Slocum said and the three nodded.

23

"Southbound stage will be here about—" The portly man behind the mustache produced a pocket watch from the red sash around his waist. "In three hours—eight fifteen."

Slocum thanked him and reined the roan around. He left the man and the half adobe, half cottonwood-log stage stop and loped for the ridge. Getting Judy and Steven on the Cheyenne stage would take some of the pressure off him. Maybe they could get on with their lives. He reined up and let the gelding blow on the crest. After the Sioux delivery to Fort Robinson he would have to drift somewhere.

The notion of doing anything about Hash's theft faded by the day, as Slocum knew full well that fool was living it up in some high-class cathouse and the gold was filtering away like water through his fingers. Oh, well—perhaps he would have memories, anyway.

He put heels to the roan and headed for the camp.

"Sounds all right," Steven said. "I guess I need to go face the music someday."

"I'll be there," Judy said. "To back you."

156

"That's the only reason I'd even go back."

She nodded and shared a look with Slocum. "He isn't reasonable we'll leave."

"And Slocum, thanks," Steven said, as if the words came hard.

Slocum dismissed his concern with a headshake. "We better mount up, we're going to make that stage."

Judy went hurriedly to thank Deering, who had returned. Slocum went for their horses. In minutes they were headed back across the sagebrush sea for the station.

When they arrived she took Slocum by the sleeve a distance away. Words came hard to her.

"I owe you some money."

"Naw, take him home. That's what you came for. I'm glad I was able to help some."

"Oh, God," she cried and clamped her hands together as if to control them. "I won't forget you. You ever come to Kansas—well, you know where we live."

He swept her up in his arms and kissed her hard on the mouth. Then he looked deep into her eyes and nodded. "Same here, girl."

"Slocum, God be with you wherever you ride."

In the crimson blast of sunset, he watched the dust trail of the Cheyenne stagecoach headed south. She'd left a notch on his heart. He wet his sun-cracked lips and turned to gather the horses.

"I've got some good whiskey inside," the stage-stop manager offered.

Slocum drew a deep breath. "That don't sound half bad."

"It ain't." Then the man laughed like a cackling hen.

Day by day Fort Robinson drew closer. Women had harvested chokecherries along the creeks. The yellowish, spotted fruit proved to be bountiful in places. Each day, the

Sioux men managed to find enough buffalo and antelope to feed the large camp.

"I'll be missing all this good meat when they're gone," O'Day said.

Slocum agreed. "So will they. Those buffalos are fast disappearing."

O'Day nodded. He dug out an old corncob pipe and loaded it. "Yeah, I can recall them herds being so wide you had to ride miles around the bunch for a day to avoid them."

"Old ways disappear like tracks."

Busy lighting his pipe, the red-faced Irishman agreed.

When they rounded the south end of the distant Black Hills that evening, Slocum went and spoke to Sleeping Bear.

"You're close enough to Fort Robinson, you won't need me any longer."

"If my people can ever help you—"

"Thanks, I'll be fine. I hope you and your people do well there."

"It will be a change. We have always lived where we wanted."

"I understand."

"You would understand. You have no home either." Sleeping Bear brought out a necklace of gold coins and held them up. "Take these and may they bring you good luck."

Slocum nodded to acknowledge them. "I have no treasure to repay you."

"The gift is from me to a brother. I need no gift, you have given me much."

Slocum took off his hat and slipped them around his neck. "Thanks." And they parted.

He met with the lieutenant in his tent a half hour later.

Deering was busy making a report and set the quill pen aside to look up at him.

"Have a chair." The officer indicated the canvas, folding one.

"I'll be riding on in the morning."

"I suspected that. The Army owes you some money for your scouting. Hell, they owe you more than that."

"I can live without it."

"Damn, I owe you. This never would have went this smoothly without your going between the two of us."

Slocum stuck out his hand and shook Deering's. "Good luck."

"I'll need it. You need anything I can ever help with, call on me."

"I will."

He left before mess the next morning. Headed northwest in the coolness of the predawn, he wondered where to start looking for Charlie Hash. The cathouses.

24

Madam Ramsey's Cathouse was a two-story house. The new whitewashed sides shone in the sun. It was quiet at that hour of the day, aside from the birds chattering in the pines around the yard. Slocum looped the reins over the rack and climbed the front stairs.

The front door was open and a black girl was mopping the polished wooden floor in the empty living room.

"Anyone up?" he asked the hatchet-assed girl.

"They be in dah kitchen."

He nodded and with his hat in his hand he walked softly in the direction she indicated. At the end of the long hall he could hear voices.

When he appeared in the doorway, the conversation went quiet. A matronly woman stood up and, with her unpainted lips pursed together, she asked, "And to whom do we owe the pleasure, sir?"

"Well, ma'am, I'm looking for an old and dear friend. Have you seen or heard of Charlie Hash?"

The handful of girls around looked at one another for the answer.

The older woman standing in the lacy robe nodded as if to say something demeaning to him for interrupting their breakfast. "Try Kate Cline's."

"Yes, ma'am. I appreciate your time."

She nodded in approval. "You do have manners but most of you rebs have them anyway. Come back when we're open for business. One of my lovely girls would like to entertain a real gentleman."

"Thanks. This Kate Cline house?"

"Big one on the left, you can't miss it."

"Thanks."

The girls at the table all smiled at him too.

He found the bigger house and climbed the stairs. He worked the doorbell that you twisted and inside a loud ringing occurred.

A girl with wild blond hair in her face, wearing only a snow-white corset, answered the door. "Come in. We ain't up this early but what can I do for you."

"Charlie Hash? I need to talk to him."

"Top of the stairs, third door on the right. But for God's sake, don't tell him I sent ya." She hitched up the corset, using both hands to save her large breasts from escaping their nest. "Get through with him, I'll give you a toss in the ole bed for two bucks."

"I might do that," he said, slipping past her and heading for the stairs.

He found the third door, eased the knob, found it unlocked and opened the door so he could slip inside the room. There on his back atop the bed, mouth open, snoring loud enough to be a sawmill and his bare chest covered in black curly hair exposed to the early light creeping in the room, slept the famous bank robber Charlie Hash.

"Get up!" Slocum said.

"Huh? Oh, my God, it's you." Hash blinked his bloodshot eyes and braced himself up on his elbows to look at Slocum.

"Where's the loot?"

Hash threw back the sheet, swung his bare legs off the bed, and went to scrubbing his beard stubble with his hands. "Well. It's like this—"

Slocum grabbed a fistful of his hair and pulled Hash's face up close to his. "I don't have all day. Where is it?"

Pained, Hash tried to winch away. "I ain't got much left."

"Get what you have and give it to me."

"You ain't going to give it back, are you?"

"Hell, it wasn't ours in the first place."

"But damn, Slocum, them express companies won't miss it. Far as they know the Injuns got it."

"Get the loot."

"I been helping these girls out that work here. Some of them got real problems in their lives and I been helping them what I kin."

Slocum nodded. "You're the big man here, I guess?"

"Well, sort of."

"Get the gold out."

"Damn," Hash swore, pulling on his pants. "You sure acting uppity law-like now."

"How must you got left?"

"Half of it—maybe . . ."

"Geez, you must have screwed every whore in Deadwood for that much money."

Hash grinned. "I been trying."

"Get the rest of the loot out."

"I hired ole Sal a good lawyer. Sent him up there to defend him too."

"Nice of you. Get the damn strongbox out."

"It's under the bed."

"You try any tricks and I'll blow you to hell and gone."

Hash held up his hands and backed away for the bed. "I won't. I swear."

Slocum dropped to his knee and, with an eye out for Hash, he jerked the strongbox out from underneath. It still felt heavy. He opened the lid and could see plenty of canvas pouches. Good, he hadn't spent all of it.

"You know, it's a terrible thing to be rich," Hash said, stretching out a holey sock. "You got so much more to worry about than you do flat broke. I thought being rich would be wonderful. But you worry all the time you're going to lose it all."

"I'll stop you worrying anymore."

"Could I have one more small pouch?"

Slocum shook his head. "Get dressed. We're taking this over to the express office."

"We are? I mean—" He swallowed hard. "We are?"

"Hell, yes, there's a reward. Even for part of it."

"But what if they think that we—I mean, they charge us with the robbery?"

"How can they?"

"Well, they must know I been here for a week or more—ah, living like I was one of them tycoons."

"They'll be damn glad to get what's left."

Hash wiped off his mouth with his hand and shook his head, putting on his shirt. "Hope it works."

When Hash was finally dressed, they carried the strongbox between them downstairs and started down the steep street in the early sun that was trying to shine down in Deadwood.

"You ever had this much money in your life?" Hash asked.

"No."

"Good, 'cause I thought I was the only one never had this much."

A clerk in a green celluloid visor was sweeping off the boardwalk in front of the Golden West Express Office—the words were in gilded letters on the front window.

"You gents want to make a deposit this morning?"

"No. We brung this back," Hash said. "Couldn't figure whose it was until someone read your name on it."

"That is one of our strongboxes. Where did you find it?"

"In an Injun camp west of here."

"Holy cow." The clerk flattened himself, holding the door open for them to come inside. "Mr. Martin! Mr. Martin! They found one of our boxes!"

Mr. Martin, in his fifties and wearing a suit and tie, cleared his throat and rose from behind his desk. He peered over and, like a man who'd been delivered a three-day-old dead coyote, looked at the battered strongbox that they set on his desk.

"Anything inside?"

"Couple dead rattlesnakes is all," Slocum said and dropped into the leather chair. Hash took the other one.

"Should I open it, sir?" the clerk asked.

"Go ahead," the man said, taking two steps back.

"They're dead," Slocum said and Hash nodded.

The clerk raised the lid and his mouth formed an *O*.

Martin stepped forward to see what had impressed his clerk and, seeing the remaining gold, smiled.

"How did you find this?"

"We took it off some warring Indians out in the Powder River country."

"What did Indians need it for?"

"To buy guns."

Martin nodded primly. "We will weigh the remaining gold, then issue you all a reward for the portion refunded."

"Me and Charlie got business elsewhere. You crack us out two hundred apiece and you can keep the rest of that reward."

"I mean, give us a little time and we can establish, I am certain, more than that."

"Two hundred's a fair figure. Right Charlie?"

"Sure."

Martin nodded his head at the clerk to go get them the money. "I want to be fair. Can I mail the rest of the reward to you?"

"Yes, send anything that's left to my cousin," Slocum said. "Judy Steward. Bender's Gap, Kansas. She'll see we get it."

"Fair enough, boys. Your honesty has paid off."

"It's about time," Hash said and stuck out his hand for his share.

Slocum looked at the tin ceiling tiles for help.

25

"Where're you going next?" Hash asked when they were out in the street.

"I guess south. Be fall up here in another six weeks and I want to be in San Anton' when the first snow hits here."

"Me too. Let me get my horse out of the livery and we'll head south together, now we're pards."

"I don't think so—"

"Aw, Slocum, you dethroned me at Kate's from being the king of the whorehouse, gave all my loot back to the Golden West Express Company and now I can't ride with you?"

"No, you can't. Spend your two hundred bucks and then go root like a hog until you find a real job."

"Helluva buddy you are. You ever find that war chief Bull Elk?"

"Naw, but he'll show up."

"Guess he will." Hash lingered while Slocum unhitched the roan. "Injuns didn't get this old horse of yours, did they?"

"No, you stole him." Slocum swung up and reined the roan around to leave.

"Hell, I had a reason. There was law after me." Hash rambled alongside Slocum's stirrup. "I don't see why we can't buddy up."

"Buddy up with someone else. I can't afford you."

Hash used his hand to deflect the bright overhead sun. "It's a shame. A damn shame. You won't take me along with you."

"Who cares," Slocum said and booted the roan into a trot.

"Wait! Wait!"

Slocum twisted in the saddle. "Why?"

"'Cause I want to go with you!"

Slocum turned back, shook his head at the shouting Hash and made the roan lope. He wanted no part of Charlie Hash ever again. He was soon in the pass above Deadwood, looking back at all the smoke from the cooking fires swirling around, obscuring part of his view of the town. On the surrounding slopes were the twisted debris of dead timber along with some live pines.

He was headed south.

26

Webber's trading post sprouted dark piles of buffalo hides. Slocum had ridden by his herd of oxen grazing out on the prairie, looked after by the old man's teenage boys. Webber took in worn-out ox for ones that were mended like so many outposts did. A two-for-one trade that even sometimes required hard cash to get the old man to swap. Somehow the tobacco-spitting, whiskered trader always came out on the long end of those deals.

Ute was his tall, straight-backed wife who spoke good English and ran the store. Folks said she had been educated back East at a church school and when she returned to the West she chose Webber for her husband since he had so many white-man things she'd come to appreciate. Of course, he had an older mate, a one-eyed Arickeria woman called Bloody Knife, who'd cut the hand off a trapper who tried to rape her. A short woman with a cloudy right eye, Bloody Knife commanded respect. The third woman in his house was a young Shoshone girl called Crazy One. Hardly older than her mid-teens, Crazy One was either nursing one of theirs or delivering another.

"If'n you ain't a pitcher for my old sore eyes," Webber shouted at the sight of Slocum. Clinging to an unpeeled pine pole that supported the sagging porch, the buckskin-clad man of fifty came hobbling across the bare ground to bear-hug Slocum.

"Damn, I've got thousands of dollars of hides up here and no one to take 'em to the gawdamn railroad. Along you come like an apparition."

"Can't help you, old hoss. I'm headed to San Anton'."

"Well, shit fire, you can deliver my hides and then go on there."

"Nope, I'm not getting caught up here and freezing my ass off another winter. I've done that before."

"Hell, come inside and drink a little fire water and we can talk. Every man has a price." He spat tobacco in the dust and waved at a boy of eight to take the roan.

"No price, Horris Webber. I'm going to Texas."

"Ute! Get the whiskey. Look who's here. My old partner, Slocum. You remember old straight-back Ute, don't you?"

Slocum nodded to her. He recalled another time when Webber had tried to bribe him to get his furs hauled and sent her to sleep with him. They never slept a wink that night in his blankets, but she did convince him to haul Webber's furs to the Missouri River. He also about froze to death that time before they got back.

"Won't work," Slocum said as the old man spat on the floor then wiped his whiskered mouth on the back of his sun-spotted hand.

"Hell, you ain't seen all my artillery yet." Webber made a sly grin and winked at Ute, who was pouring whiskey in the tin cups for them.

"Bottle and bond," the trader bragged, hugging Ute around the waist as she stood beside him holding the bottle. "I ain't feeding you no damn old Injun hootch."

"Whiskey, women, bribes—won't work this time—" Slocum held his hands up to restrain the man. "I ain't hauling no hides to the railroad for you or anyone."

"Good enough, I won't ask you again. 'Cept if you change your mind about it—well, I'd sure pay you well."

"No deal."

"Fine." Webber raised his tin cup and toasted. "To our making some money."

"To you figuring out how else to get them there." Slocum clanged his cup against the trader's.

"When did you eat last?"

"Day before."

"Our guest is starved," Webber said to Ute.

She agreed, put the bottle on the table and left the main room, which was piled high with trade goods and more expensive pelts hanging on every rafter and post.

"You ever seen a white wolf?" Webber asked as he watched Slocum twist around to view everything. "Got one. Snow-white albino. Rare dude."

"Worth a lot?"

"Worth plenty. The Injun woman skinned it out careful and it can be mounted. Figure it's worth a thousand in New York."

Slocum drank some more whiskey. Webber probably paid five dollars in trade goods to the woman for the skin. But that was how he made his money. Buy cheap, sell high and he was one of the few that existed out there.

Ute showed him to a small cabin after he had a big meal.

"You recall the time we spent going to the Missouri?" he asked, looking around the room as she lit the lamp.

"I never had so much fun." Shaking out the match, she straightened her stiff back. Her full bustline filled the beaded buckskin blouse and he recalled what they looked like. Long and subtle, firm to his touch. "And I also recall we about froze too."

They both laughed.

"You must excuse me. I must go and wait on the customers. I run the store now. The others can't count. They know nothing."

"Thank you, Ute, I will be fine. A night's sleep in that bed and I'll be a new man."

She nodded that she understood. "Sleep good. You make my husband laugh. He doesn't laugh enough."

He followed her to the doorway and after watching the swirl of the long elk-skin fringe whipping her shapely calves he slow-like closed the door. Some woman—that Ute.

He undid the gun belt and hung it on the chair back close to the bed. Then he sat and removed his boots and breathed out a gush of relief with each. Vest undone and his kerchief hung over the holster, he undid his shirt— thinking about Judy and hoping she had reached Bender's Gap safely. His belt unlatched, he hung his britches on the other side of the ladder chair.

How long had it been since he had slept in a bed? Weeks, months? He stretched out on his back, wiggling to find the most comfort for his stiff back muscles, and gazed at the underside of the shingle roof in the growing darkness. In the arms of the seductive mattress, he fell deeply asleep.

Far, far away, a hot mouth worked on his growing erection. The eagerness of her actions made him squirm, her small fingers cupping his scrotum and then gently individually squeezing his balls as if testing him. Her fiery mouth and tongue ravaged the head of his dick the whole time.

Half awake, he felt the pleasure from her actions draw a smile to the corners of his sun-blistered lips. Then he reached down, expecting to find his throbbing erection standing like a flagpole. Instead he touched braids and a woman's head. He bolted up in the dark room.

"Who are you?" He knew it was not Ute. This woman was much smaller.

She sat up in the starlight and wiped her mouth on the back of her hands. In the shadowy light, he could see she was on her knees and naked. The starlight shone on her pear-shaped breasts and the lines across her flat belly.

"Antelope is my name."

"What the hell you doing in here?"

She giggled. "You don't know?"

"I don't mean that—why are you here?"

Her hand slid in and grasped his stiff shaft at the base. "Do we talk forever?"

"No," he said and grinned back at her.

She let go and moved to get beside him. Her firm breasts dragged over his arm as she slithered by him, snakelike, to lie on the mattress at his side.

He moved to get between her legs and she raised her knees. His aching skin-tight dick entered her slowly. She raised her butt off the bed to ease his admission. In short jabs he was soon at her ring and when he forced the head past her restraint she cried out. With each plunge into her, he wanted to shout out loud, "Hee-yah oxen!" Damn that Webber, anyway—where in the hell did he find her at?

27

A cold wind from the north made Slocum hunch the heavy buffalo coat up higher on his neck and shoulders. Icy crystals carried on the sharp wind struck his cheeks and he ducked his head to make the fifty yards to the cabin. Damn this Nebraska winter anyway—they were waiting for a break in the weather that usually came in November or early December to make the last trip to Ogallala and the railroad.

Webber had six more double wagonloads of hides he wanted delivered on the winter market. With a seventh double wagon to carry grain and forage for the ox teams, they should make the trip easy—if the weather would cooperate. But it had no plans to please them soon so he could come back with the last hides. He went in the cabin and the room's warmth struck him in the face. The heat began to burn the frostbitten skin on his cheeks as Antelope helped him out of the robe.

"You may have to wait until spring to take them down there," she said, looking out the window made from glass bottles in a row.

Standing on her toes, she frowned at whatever she saw in the post yard.

"What is it?"

"Some Indians, they look in bad shape. Come see for yourself."

He looked through the flying moths of ice and snow. Women, some holding children, staggered along with thin horses pulling a travois. They looked cold and hungry.

"You think they are more wild ones going to Fort Robinson?" she asked.

"Probably. But they have four days' travel to get there."

"My father will give them food on credit." She wrinkled her nose at him to dismiss any concern. "Take off your clothes. You can do nothing more about the wagons or cattle today. You will be mine in the bed all afternoon."

"We better not, Bloody Hand is coming to see us."

"Why her?" Antelope stood on her toes to see the short woman coming all wrapped in a trade blanket. A peeved look on her face, she went to the door and let the woman in before she could knock.

"What is wrong?"

"Father want him come quick." She pointed a stark finger at Slocum.

"What for?" Antelope asked, acting perturbed by the woman's demand.

Slocum gave her braids a toss and smiled at the one-eyed woman. "Tell him I am coming."

"Good, gawdamn Sioux anyway." She went out the door, wrapping herself in the blanket and hurried across the white ground.

"Why did she say—gawdamn Sioux? They Sioux?"

"I guess," Slocum said, putting on the buffalo jacket again and bending over to kiss her on his way out.

"Be careful," she said and closed the door behind him.

He passed several hard-eyed Indians on the porch and found the store crowded with more. One was lying on top of the stack of deer hides. A big man, his face wrinkled and though he looked very sick and had been for a while, he looked familiar.

"Reckon what he's got is contagious?" Webber asked, spitting on the floor. The patient coughed and it racked his entire body.

"Might be—I ain't a doc. He needs one bad, to my notion."

"They give up on Indian remedies. Taking him to Robinson."

"That's best."

"I'll give them some food and get them going. Don't need no more diseases around here. You know him, don't you?"

"No."

"Yes, you do, that's Bull Elk."

"Really?"

Webber nodded and shouted to Ute behind the counter. "Give them some slabs of salt pork, couple hundred pounds of corn meal and every child a piece of hard candy."

"You gawdamn good sumbitch—Webber," an old Indian said to him and the others nodded. Soon the word spread and a woman began to clap her hands over her head. The *hi-ho* singing began as they carried the provisions out of the store. They left dancing, their rawhide soles scratching the worn floor. Four women carried the semiconscious war chief out on his stretcher, careful to cover him before they went outside.

Already women were putting up poles for their tepees to the side of the post yard. Slocum could see some feeding small handfuls of the precious ground corn to their gaunt horses.

Webber looked past Slocum at them and at last grunted in disgust before he turned back. "Ute, tell Matt to run that crippled steer down there for them to eat."

The woman nodded.

28

The weather broke. The thermometer rose to thirty-eight degrees and Slocum hitched four teams to each wagon unit. Already loaded with skins and provisions, they left for Nebraska before dawn.

"It thaws too much we may fall it through," Bleu Champeau warned.

Slocum agreed and then told the man to get going or he'd be late. His teamsters consisted of three Frenchmen, Champeau, Fernando and Capaz, a black, Mathew, a breed called Caw and a six foot six Osage named Big Man. The trip in the fall had gone smoothly enough. The teamsters griped a lot but that was their nature. Anyone who drove oxen, day in and day out, was bound to become exasperated at the entire world. Mules were unruly, hard mouthed, stubborn and even flighty, but beside oxen to haul freight they were angelic animals. In first place came powerful workhorses, but they couldn't live on dead grasses and pull the loads these cattle did day after day. Still, cracking a whip over dull oxen was so much like an act of futility that by the end of the day the teamsters were ready to fight each other for some simple response.

176

Iron rims creaked across the prairie, not ever as flat as described in geography book. Men drove uphill all day wondering why they had such problems and never discovered the grade until they reached the peak late in the day—some twelve miles from the night before's camp, behind in the deep vale.

Slocum watched the feathery clouds roll in at supper time. Champeau forecast bad blizzards. Mathew thought light snow. Big Man ate, grunted and farted until everyone moved upwind of him to eat the venison Slocum had shot earlier that day for them. No one complained too much to a six foot six full-blood.

Snow came and went. They found good forage that was not snow covered and rested the animals for a day there to eat their fill. Then they yoked up and slugged on toward Ogallalla.

Christmas Eve, Slocum passed around two bottles of Webber's precious whiskey that Ute had slipped him before they left. He laughed, pouring some in his tin cup.

"Any man mentions us drinking this good whiskey to Webber will get his ass kicked up between his shoulders."

His words drew a big hurrah and they toasted to one another's health. That evening especially he wished he'd had Antelope to share his robes, but the trip was tough enough on everyone. Besides, these men pissed whenever they had to, wherever they were and had the manners of billy goats.

New Years came and went under the stars and the cry of hungry wolves. The year 1878 rolled in on a blinding snowstorm by midday. Slocum saw the huge goose-gray wall bearing down on them. They went into camp early and remained there for the next forty-eight hours while the winds tore at them.

January 12th, they crossed the Platt River Bridge and Slocum paid all the men an advance of thirty dollars prom-

ised them after the animals were put up and cared for. He
went to the nearest café and ate a huge steak and some potatoes. Then he went to the mercantile, bought new socks,
wool underwear, canvas pants and a thick wool shirt. After
that he crossed the snow-rutted street to the barbershop for
a shave, haircut and bath.

His nose full of talcum powder, he waded through the
white stuff another block to the Palace Hotel, got a room,
climbed the stairs, fell in bed and went to sleep, he hoped
forever.

"Don't make a move!" someone said in his ear.

He couldn't see them. The three had a lamp and guns on
him. But he recalled that voice—Piper had found him.

Seeing it was still dark outside, he wondered how long
he had managed to sleep. Damn, what would they do next?
No telling.

"Get dressed, we're taking you to the local jail. Then
we'll put you on the train for Lodge Pole."

"I never robbed that bank."

"Well, I'd say you won't get as smart a lawyer as your
partner got to defend him."

"Oh?"

"Yeah, he smooth-talked them jurors plumb out of them
charges."

"We figured he must of cost you boys all you got out of
that bank," the Kid said.

"Shut up," Piper ordered.

No way that Hash would ever get his hands on that kind
of money again. He'd have to do what he could for himself.
Those teamsters were up to their eyeballs in pussy and
drinking, no way . . .

He knew he should never have let Webber talk him into
doing that teamster business. Lovely as Antelope was . . .

He drew a deep breath dressing under the muzzle of two guns. The trader had his skins down there to be loaded on the train—and all he had to do was go face a trial for a crime he'd never committed. Tough hand to play out.

They hustled him down to the jail. It was a cold building and Slocum felt grateful he had his buffalo coat to wear. They locked him in a cell by himself in a row of them with guys huddling around trying to keep warm. The cries for more heat went unheeded and Slocum curled up on an iron bench to catch some more sleep.

He awoke to the sound of tinkling glass overhead and a Frenchman calling, "You in dere, Slo-cum?"

"Yeah," he shouted and jumped up as he saw the Frenchman put a large log inside the bars. A chain was wrapped around it and someone outside went, "heeyah!"

The guy in the next cell came over and grasped the bars. "What the hell they doing?"

"I think modifying the jail."

Things began to crack and pop. Dust from the mortar began to fly and the entire wall began to cave outward.

"Oh, shit," one prisoner hollered. "We'll really be cold, now!"

Slocum leaped over the rubble and a giant hand caught him by the shoulder. His heart stopped. So close to being away and . . . He glanced up and Big Man handed him the reins to a saddled horse.

"You ride."

"Yes," he agreed. He stepped in the saddle and gave a loud *"Hee-yah!"*

He crossed the Platt River Bridge, hooves drumming in the starry night. Three days and two other horses later, he was at Webber's Post, sitting in a captain's chair and talking to the man.

"Your hides are down there. The men can handle it. Except they may have to pay for a new jail wall if they can prove they did it."

"I pay for that. So you must go."

"Yeah, Piper will be on my tracks already."

"You tell Antelope yet?"

"She's next."

Webber scratched his right ear. "You come back. Always have work for you. Need money you send word, huh? I see the Piper, I cut his balls off." He sliced the air with the side of his hand.

"I'll need a fresh horse in the morning. Take it out of my pay."

"No! I pay you and give you a good gray horse."

"I don't—"

"Don't argue. You can't go south. Where you go?"

"I'll swing west to Cheyenne and down that way on the Texas trail."

"Be a good idea."

"I better go tell her."

Webber squirmed uncomfortably in the chair. "I rather go fight a grizzly."

Slocum grinned at him. Wasn't far from the truth.

"Oh, you hear?"

"What?"

"Bull Elk died."

He would not miss him.

29

Grateful for the weak sun, Slocum headed the fresh gray horse Webber had given him southwest. His breath came in great clouds of moisture. His notion was to swing by Cheyenne then take the Texas cattle trail down the Kansas-Colorado line and make his way south from the panhandle. Visions of the warm sun on the courtyards of San Anton' danced in his head as he looked at the small patches of snow in the shade of the low-growing sagebrush. Like the tawny-skinned señoritas with hips that swayed and firm breasts that shook at him, they waited for his return down there in Bexar County. Even the music found his ears, wrapped in a woolen scarf—castanets and guitars played his song. He should hate Webber for even coaxing him into staying up there—but the fresh recall of his daughter Antelope's sensuous body, her oneness and seductive ways—damn, to ride off and leave her had not been easy.

But Piper would find him if he remained at the trading post. A word in a bar from some half-drunk teamster, a loose tongue blabbing to some whore and Piper would find the source and come on a fast horse. No, he better move south and get lost in the Lone Star State.

That night he didn't bother to build a fire. He hobbled the gray after finding some nonfrozen water in a spring at the base of a bluff. Wrapped in his blankets and clothing, he hoped he wouldn't freeze to death while he slept. But lurking wolves woke him and he shot at their silhouettes, sending them, stung by his lead and yelping, off in the night.

A new day rolled in on a blinding snowstorm and by midday he was forced to wait it out in a draw. He rode on after that.

The next afternoon he found cattle and a rider. The two reined up on their horses, face-to-face.

"You're a far piece from Texas," Slocum said to the boy, who called himself Davie.

"I ever get back there I damn sure ain't coming up here again and freezing my balls off for no thirty and found."

"Your outfit needing some help?"

"Yeah, Joe broke his leg and a week ago Curly left during the night. I bet ole Fuzzy would hire you."

"Fuzzy, the ramrod?"

"Yeah, he's the man. I'll ride along with you. I've done seen enough stock for today. This country always this cold?"

"Sure is, this is a warm spell. Why I don't usually stay up here."

"Smart idea."

The Diamond T had used an abandoned sod-buster shack for headquarters. They'd dragged up poles to build some makeshift corrals. Even had a stack of hay for the horses they kept up. When Slocum dismounted at the hitch-rail, Davie rode on to put up his horse.

"Get inside. Too cold out here to talk," a short man wrapped in a blanket said from the half-open door. His pointed chin bristled with snowy whiskers. He closed the door after his quick words.

The interior was devoid of the eternal wind. Dimly lit by smoky tallow candles, it smelled of horse sweat, saddle leather, tobacco and cooked fatback. More like a cave than a house. Still, the warmth swept Slocum's face and burned the cold surface like a searing fire.

"Needing work?" Fuzzy asked.

"I could use some."

"Who you worked for?"

"Some small outfits. Took some herds up the trail to Abilene."

"I never ask a man his business. But you been shaved and had a haircut real recent like. A man don't leave them comforts looking for puncher's thirty and found less'n he's got a good reason." Fuzzy held up his hands. "I don't give a damn why. Just make trouble elsewhere. You savvy?"

"I savvy good. I won't be no trouble to you."

Fuzzy nodded. "That's Joe, laid up over there. Broke his leg in a horse wreck. We set it best we could. It'll heal. He's a little grouchy. Like an old bear. Me and the kid you come in with—Davie—we make wide circles as we can around him.

"Curly left out a week ago. Never said a word, got up one morning, found him and his gear weren't here. Took a ranch horse but I owed him enough pay would have covered it. He had some sweet Mormon gal on his mind."

Slocum nodded, grateful to be out of the heavy buffalo coat and inside—away from the talons of winter.

Each day, he and Davie made short circles, each in opposite directions, driving cattle back toward the headquarters so they didn't stray too far. Bad days they stayed at the cabin. Once a week they dragged in firewood from horseback to supplement the bin full of dry cow chips. Sawing it and then splitting it ate up their bad weather days.

Six weeks passed and the weather tempered, but Slocum warned them winter wasn't through in that country till mid-May.

"My gawd, that's three months away," Davie said.

Silent Joe got so he could hobble out to the woodpile and he soon took over the wood preparation. That gave the two riders more time to go farther out looking for wood.

Slocum had ridden to the base of the hills, searching for strays. With no success, he had started back when he saw them—three bucks on horseback on the high ground. They immediately turned off and went under the far lip, out of sight. He was over fifteen miles from camp. The shaggy Texas mustang had been eating some fine-cured hay—some sod-buster had charged Fuzzy seven dollars a ton for the feed. The Indian ponies probably had been feasting on willow bark, hardly a nutritious forage. But the distance was a big factor.

Skin crawling on the back of his neck under his kerchief, he set the bay in a trot for camp. Fastest he could get there would be two hours, maybe three. He still had four hours of daylight left in the winter-shortened day, but war parties liked the three-to-one odds. He soon made the bay lope.

When he looked back, he saw no sign of them. That meant nothing. They could be riding parallel to him and out of sight over any rise. Would they try to cut him off before he reached the headquarters? Funny thing, though Injuns were on his mind, neither he nor the rest of the crew had ever spoke of them once. The country they were in was on the edge of the most hostile tribes still out on the loose, but whether they hadn't spoken about them out of fear of bad luck or were simply trying to avoid talking period, Slocum was uncertain.

Maybe Curly was the only smart one for leaving. Then Slocum saw the black finger of smoke straight ahead of him. Too late. His heart sank. The hostiles had taken the headquarters and he'd better make new plans. Too late to save Fuzzy and Joe. He hoped that Davie had seen the telltale smoke in time and ridden on too.

Two days later, Slocum stumbled into Fort Fetterman on the North Fork of the Laramie River. An orderly helped him off his horse and half carried him into the officer of the day's office.

"What happened?" the captain asked.

"Injuns got the Diamond T bunch." Then Slocum's world went dark and he never awoke again until he looked into the eyes of an angel.

"I'm Mrs. Taylor. Dr. Taylor's wife. I see you finally woke up. You must have been in the saddle a long time."

"Two days, I think."

"I have some bad news. They found the others dead at the burned-out place."

"Two or three dead?"

"Three," the attractive brunette said with a pleasant smile as she put a cool washcloth on his forehead. "Your fever has finally broken."

He felt grubby underneath the stiff-starched sheets and blankets but for the first time in a long while his body parts were warm all over.

"They telegraphed the owners in Texas. You know them?"

"No, ma'am. I'd just hired on a month ago."

"When their man gets up here he may want to know lots from you about the herd."

Slocum nodded. He had no plans to be there. One thing he knew for certain, if she didn't leave the room soon his bladder was going to bust.

30

He could regret lots of things. The loss of the gray horse to the Injuns' raid on the Diamond T was the main thing. The head-slinging bay tried hard to buck him off when he saddled him to leave Fort Fetterman. Fueled up by a week of the Army's hay and corn, the shaggy-maned bronc made some high dives under him out in the dry powdery snow. He drew the shouts of several troopers who rushed from the barns to see the grand show.

Whipping him across from side to side with the reins, Slocum tore out of the fort grounds headed for Cheyennne. He had no time for the pony's foolishness. Besides, if he stayed in the outpost a day longer, he'd have to make a move on the doctor's attractive wife. Somehow, she'd become too close to him, fussing over him so personally even after he had recovered, so he rode out to avoid contact with her. Though he had imagined her mature body under the starched dresses, buttoned to the throat, which were only a guise for a hot-blooded woman who really wanted to be stark naked before him and taken wantonly.

He closed his eyes to the too-bright sun and lashed the horse again for attempting to act up.

Two days later, he saw a green sheep wagon and two barking collies, and soon the busty figure of Myrtle Brown appeared in the doorway.

"Why if it ain't ole Slocum. What brings you back here? Get off that wooly pony and come inside before you freeze your plumbing off."

Like darting moths, snowflakes whirled around his face. The thick clouds had tried all day to get going, and it looked in late afternoon like they'd finally get busy. He stripped the saddle off as the short horse shook the bushy mane that fell on both sides of his neck. After he put on the hobbles so the bay wouldn't leave for Texas, he slipped the curb bit out of his mouth and turned him loose.

His boots on the steps made the wagon rock. He stepped inside the small trailer and she handed him a cup of steaming coffee. The warmth set in quickly as she helped him out of his heavy outer clothing.

"Well, sit down there and tell me where the hell you've been and what all's happened since I seen you last."

"You got a couple of hours?"

"For you darling, I've got days." She smiled big and he could see the inviting deep cleavage between her breasts.

"Good. I left here last summer headed for Deadwood . . ."

Watch for

SLOCUM'S GOLD MOUNTAIN

315th novel in the exciting SLOCUM series
from Jove

Coming in May!